FELL IN Love WITH AN EARL

ANNA BRADLEY

OLIVER HEBER BOOKS

CHAPTER
ONE

He'd lost his hat somewhere between London and Hawke's Run. Of the dozen different things now trying Adrian's temper, it was the lost hat that made it snap.

An elegant hat, polished boots and a flawless white cravat—tied in *Trone d'Amour*, and artfully creased—separated a fashionable London gentleman from a plain country squire. He'd given up his left boot and his cravat as lost before he'd left the city last night, the latter being covered in vomit, and the former...well, he wasn't entirely sure what had happened to his boot, but it wasn't on his foot. He must have lost it when Lady Pamela shoved him out the window.

But a gentleman's hat—that was one step too bloody far. A beaver hat was a precious, hallowed thing. Akin to a holy relic, for God's sake.

Practical, too.

He ventured a glance into the merciless glare above, wincing as pain lanced his skull and hard, white sunlight seared his eyeballs. Was it necessary for it to shine *quite* so brightly? He'd happily give up

1

his one remaining boot for a comforting layer of London smog. Really, it was just this sort of unreasonable cheerfulness that made people detest the country.

Here, in particular.

If he'd known when he left his townhouse last night that he'd find himself *here*, he'd have downed a whole bottle of brandy instead of half, but it was too bloody late now. Sobriety had caught up to him somewhere near Hoddesdon, which was a great pity, as he preferred to remain as close to unconscious as possible whenever he was in the vicinity of Hawke's Run.

Damned if anyone who saw him right now would recognize him as the fashionable, charming Lord Hawke. He looked far closer to the dissipated barbarian he actually was, and that *smell*. Stale smoke, regurgitated brandy, and the thick, cloying stench of Lady Pamela's perfume.

Taken together, it was enough to make him...

He gagged, bile burning his throat, but he choked it back before it spewed from his lips and splashed into his lap. He reined in his horse at the end of the drive and waited until his stomach ceased its rebellion before running the tip of his tongue cautiously over his parched lips.

This was no time to cast up his accounts. He was about to appear at his country estate after...six, or was it seven? long months of unexplained absence, and he was reeking of wicked deeds as it was. Breeches splattered with vomit was doing it a bit too brown—

"Oh, dear. This *is* a conundrum."

The soft exclamation came out of nowhere, startling him into another ill-fated glance into the remorseless sky above. He caught a glimpse of bare, dark branches clawing at the blue, and a flash of something yellow. It wasn't the sun this time. A remarkably large bird, then? He bloody well hoped not, as any bird such an aggressive shade of yellow was sure to be a vicious predator.

He snapped his eyes shut to prevent his retinas from bursting into flames, but they flew open again when something sharp struck him in the face. "What the *devil*?" He despised the country, yes, but this was the first sign he'd ever had it despised him in return.

"Oh, no. That wasn't meant to happen."

This time he took the precaution of shading his eyes with his hand before glancing up. He could see nothing but shifting shadows at first, but as his vision adjusted, he caught a glimpse of the hem of a shockingly yellow cloak and a slender foot clad in a worn half-boot dangling from one of the branches above his head. "No? You mean to say you *don't* make a habit of hurling branches at innocent travelers?"

Or guilty ones, as the case may be.

"It wasn't a branch, but a clump of mistletoe." The foot swung back and forth. "Rather a large clump. I do beg your pardon. How unfortunate you're not wearing a hat."

He gritted his teeth at the mention of his missing hat. "If I'd known I'd be attacked, madam, I'd have worn a suit of armor."

She laughed. *Laughed*, as if this were all tremendously amusing. The sound echoed in the crisp morning air like birdsong, the cheerful chirp of it scraping over his raw nerves and further souring his temper. His jaw clenched. "What do you mean, hanging about in that tree like a bloody monkey?"

She gave a prim little sniff. "There's no need to curse, sir."

"I beg to differ, madam. How did you even manage to climb up there?" It was a large tree, at least thirty feet tall.

"Why, the same way anyone climbs a tree. One limb at a time."

"Well, come down from there at once."

"As happy as I'd be to oblige you, sir, I'm afraid it's not that simple. I'm, er...attached, you see."

"Attached? What do you mean?"

There was a brief pause, then the delicate clearing of a throat. "Attached means joined, sir, or fastened, or connected to—"

"For God's sake, I know what attached means! I meant to inquire as to the nature of your particular attachment to that tree." Good Lord, wasn't that obvious?

"Oh. I beg your pardon. You just seemed, ah...a bit confused. It's my hair. It's gotten tangled in one of the branches, and I can't get it loose. I'm stuck."

"Nonsense," he huffed. "You're not stuck. Simply scamper back down the way you went up. Cats do it all the time."

"Cats don't have long hair that is apt to get tangled in the branches. Young ladies do, however, and I am, alas, the latter rather than the former. Unfortunate, but there it is."

"Untangle it, then." It wouldn't prove to be that easy, of course, because things were never as easy as they should be, and because he'd clearly stumbled into the ninth circle of hell.

Or Hawke's Run. Same bloody thing.

"Untangle it?" She made a sound like a hastily-smothered snort. "That *is* an inspired idea, sir. Indeed, I wonder I didn't think of it myself. But now that I consider it, it occurs to me that if I release my hold on the trunk, I'm quite likely to tumble out of the tree. So, you see, I'm in a bit of a quandary."

First a conundrum, and now a quandary? This chit was making his head throb. "You are indeed, and I've half a mind to leave you in it. You were foolish enough to climb up there. Had I not had the cursed bad luck to stumble upon you, you'd have had to get yourself down somehow."

He waited, but his threat did not have the effect he'd intended. Any woman in her right mind would have dissolved into a flood of tears and pleas for his assistance, but she only said, "Do as you will, then. I'll find my own way down eventually."

He cast a despairing glance from his unbooted foot to the frozen ground below. Absurd chit. It would serve her right if he abandoned her to her fate, but as much as she deserved to lose her toes to frostbite for her ridiculous stunt, he couldn't quite bring himself to leave her up there. Good Lord, how he loathed heroics. "Stay where you are. I'll climb up and untangle you."

"Your gallantry does you credit, sir."

He grunted. She was doing her best to sound grateful, but there was a distinct thread of amusement in her voice. "Gallantry be damned. I simply choose not to explain to the magistrate how some witless girl froze to death in my tree."

Her foot stopped swinging. "*Your* tree?"

"My tree, my branches, and my mistletoe." He dis-

5

mounted and picked his way across the rutted drive, trying to sidestep the patches of frozen mud, but it was difficult with only one boot, and by the time he reached the bottom of the tree his stocking was ruined. Not that it made much difference, at this point. "You're trespassing on *my* property, madam."

"Your property," she repeated, her amusement vanishing. "If this is your property, then you must be—"

"Adrian Chatham, the Earl of Hawke. If I fall from the tree and perish from a broken neck, you'll have the satisfaction of knowing the earl was killed in service to *you*."

He waited, but she didn't offer another impertinent reply, so he started climbing. He paused when he was level with her foot and squinted up at her. "On which side are you tangled?"

"The left. There's a thick branch just there, right by your—"

"Yes, yes. I see it." He wedged his foot between two sturdy branches, wrapped his arms around a bough above him and swung himself up. The limb gave a protesting groan, and he shook his head to dislodge the image of his twisted body lying unconscious under this cursed tree with bits of his skull scattered about, and kept climbing until he reached a limb that could take his weight, several branches above and behind her.

The dappled sunlight filtering through the trees lit up a thick mass of wild, golden-brown curls, because of course, she must have wild curls like some heroine from a romantic novel.

Impertinent, somehow, that hair.

He couldn't see her face, but in her yellow cloak,

6

with that irrepressible hair wound around the branches she looked like some sort of exotic tree nymph. The thought irritated him more than it should have, and his voice was gruff when he asked, "Why would you climb a tree with your hair unbound?"

"I didn't." She held up a wide blue ribbon. "Why would you go riding with only one boot?"

"I didn't." He braced himself against the branch at his back. "I was, er...separated from it. In any case, it's not the same thing."

"No," she agreed. "I didn't *lose* my ribbon."

"I didn't lose my boot, either." Not exactly. It was likely still lodged between the window and the sill in Lady Pamela's dressing room. "But I have no intention of explaining myself to a thief who climbed my tree to steal my mistletoe."

"Steal it! I would *never*—"

"Quiet, if you please, madam. I'm rather busy." His hands hovered over the nest of curls and branches, but he hesitated, reluctant to touch her. He didn't want to know if her hair was as thick and soft as it looked.

He hadn't any choice, however, unless he wanted to spend the rest of his days in this god-forsaken tree with her. "Hold still, now." He reached for her, his fingertips catching in her heavy curls as he began to work her hair free from the branches, one lock at a time.

She stiffened when he first touched her, but she did as he bade her, keeping silent and still. It seemed to take ages, and by the time he was finished he was desperate to stop touching her. "There. You're free."

As soon as he'd untangled the last lock and slid

his hands free of her hair, she scampered down the tree, hopping from branch to branch as quick and agile as a monkey, the sun caressing her shiny curls. "Thank you, my lord."

He followed at a more cautious pace. Getting down a tree in one boot was a devil of a business, as it turned out. By the time he reached the bottom, she'd gathered up the clumps of mistletoe she'd liberated from the branches above.

"Making away with your ill-gotten gains, are you?" He crossed his arms over his chest and leaned against the tree. "What in the world are you going to do with all that mistletoe?"

"It's for the St. Mary's Ladies' Benevolent Society's Christmas fete. We're, ah...well, we'd planned to make kissing balls to decorate Goodall Abbey. The monies raised from the fete benefit the church fund, you know, but if you object to giving your mistletoe to the cause, we can always—"

"Take it. Never let it be said I don't support the church. Or kissing." Between the missing boot and hat and the stench wafting from him, he was far from being the charming gentleman who beguiled London's beauties, but he was rather proud of this little bit of gallantry.

Alas, it was utterly wasted on her. She didn't even appear to hear him, so preoccupied was she with stuffing the mistletoe into the pockets of the outrageous yellow cloak she was wearing. He'd never seen a more ridiculous garment in his life, but either she didn't realize it, or she didn't care, and thus she carried it off in a way few ladies could have done. "May I have the pleasure of knowing who hurled my own mistletoe at my head this morning?"

"Nonsense. I never hurled anything." She raised her face to his, cocking her head. "Are you always this cross, my lord?"

Her face was not what he'd been expecting. She wasn't a great beauty, exactly—her generous mouth and pointed chin defied any claim to it—but hers was the sort of face that fascinated.

Her eyes were wide, thickly-lashed and an unusual clear, grayish blue. Not the glittering, dark blue of sapphires, or the gray of storm clouds, but something in between the two, rather like...oh, he didn't bloody know. Blueberries? No, that wasn't it. Winter frost, perhaps?

He'd never seen eyes like hers before, but then Hawke's Run was a place of *never befores* and *never agains*.

Everything about her, from her full red lips to the high arch of her cheekbones to the spattering of freckles across the bridge of her nose so arrested him it was as if the bright sun had once again scorched his eyeballs.

She must have noticed him staring, but it didn't seem to trouble her. She merely raised her chin and met his eyes. "How do you do, Lord Hawke? I'm Miss Helena Templeton."

Helena Templeton? The last name sounded vaguely familiar. Hadn't he heard some gossip about some chit or other with the surname Templeton? Yes, there'd been something, but he couldn't recall what exactly, and the first name hadn't been Helena, in any case.

So, who the devil was she, and what was she doing up his tree? "Who?"

Her brows drew together. "Miss Helena Templeton. Your sons' governess, my lord?"

"Nonsense. I don't employ a governess." Certainly not one who was as much trouble as her. He'd sooner lay his neck upon a chopping block than permit such an impertinent chit in his house. Anyone could see the girl was trouble, and he had enough of that already. As for her distracting face and unusual eyes, he didn't *want* to be fascinated by them, or by her.

He simply wanted peace.

"I assure you that you do indeed employ a governess, Lord Hawke. I've been here these past six months now. Your boys are a delight. I'm tremendously fond of them."

Ryan and Etienne, a delight? Now he knew she was lying. He loved his sons, but he'd yet to hear any governess describe them as delightful. Though if she really was their governess, it would explain why she was up that tree. They'd likely chased her up there, and even now were watching from the windows to see if she'd find her way back down.

God knew it would be easy enough for them to intimidate a petite, slender thing like her. The boys were young yet, only six years old, but they were wild, just as he'd been at their age, and then there were two of them. It wouldn't take much for them to overwhelm her.

It seemed it was time to have a word with his housekeeper, Mrs. Norris. "Go on back up to the house, Miss Templeton. You're dismissed for now."

"Of course, my lord." She offered him a curtsy. "Welcome home, Lord Hawke."

"No need to trouble yourself with the courtesies, Miss Templeton." He swung back up into the saddle with as much grace as a man missing a boot and his hat could summon, and peered down at her. "I won't be here long enough for it to make any difference."

She didn't reply, and he didn't spare another word for her, but jerked his horse's head toward the castle and thundered up the drive without a backward glance.

CHAPTER
TWO

Helena wandered up the drive toward the castle in Lord Hawke's wake, her pockets filled with prickly bunches of glossy green mistletoe, her head still ringing from the wicked curses that had just spilled from his lordship's lips into her unsuspecting ears.

Such a prodigious quantity of them, and in such quick succession, too!

He was a bit, er...well, she'd been expecting someone a trifle more...that is, the rumors she'd heard of him hadn't been to his credit, certainly, but she hadn't imagined he'd be *quite* so...

Oh, for pity's sake. There was no sense dancing about it.

He was a perfect beast. Growly, ill-tempered, rude, and unforgivably arrogant for a man without a hat, a cravat, or a decent pair of boots.

Didn't employ a governess, indeed! It was as plain as day he hadn't the vaguest idea who she was. Even after she'd told him her name, he'd merely stared blankly at her, as if he'd never heard of such a thing as a governess before.

On the bright side, he didn't seem to have heard of a Templeton sister, either, which was fortunate, indeed, given all the gossip about them and their al-legedly magical matchmaking schemes.

But really, did Lord Hawke imagine his six-year-old sons cared for themselves? Or had he forgotten them entirely? One didn't like to think any father could be capable of such a thing, but she'd been the governess here for six months, and this was the first time she'd ever laid eyes on Lord Hawke.

He was not, alas, a shining example of paternal devotion.

She threw open one of the massive, iron-studded double doors that led into the castle with a bit more force than necessary, and hurried through the en-tryway and downstairs into the kitchens. "Good morning, Abby."

Abigail Hurley, the castle's kitchen maid was seated at the table, reading over cook's notes from a scrap of paper, a tiny silver kitten perched on her shoulder. She looked up with a smile as Helena en-tered. "Morning, miss."

Helena passed through the kitchen into the still-room beyond, unloaded the contents of her pockets into a basket waiting on the end of the long work ta-ble, then returned to the kitchen, pausing in front of the fire to rub the chill from her hands. "So, Abby. What can you tell me about the Earl of Hawke?"

Abby didn't look up from her note. "What, you mean our mysterious employer? *That* Earl of Hawke?"

"Not so mysterious anymore." Helena set the kettle on the stove to boil. "He's returned to Hawke's Run. I saw him myself just now, coming up the drive."

Abby's head jerked up, her eyes bulging. "The Earl

of Hawke! What, you mean to say the *Earl of Hawke* is here?"

"Is there another earl I'm not aware of?" Goodness, she hoped not. A single earl was more than enough for one morning, and the Earl of Hawke enough for an entire lifetime.

"Nay, miss, it's just...his lordship, here?" Abby leapt up, wincing as the kitten hung on, digging its claws into her shoulder. "I beg your pardon, Hestia, but Lord Hawke's return is the most exciting thing that's happened in Hawke's Run since...well, ever."

"Give Hestia here." Helena held out her hands for the kitten.

Abby disentangled Hestia, pressed an absent kiss on the kitten's fluffy head, then handed her over. "That must be why Mrs. Norris just flew out of here like her hair was on fire."

"Likely as not. I daresay Lord Hawke summoned her." He didn't seem like the patient sort, either.

"And you say you *saw* him? Really, miss, it's terribly unfair that all the most delightful things should always happen to *you*."

"It wasn't delightful in the least, Abby. I was stuck in that enormous alder tree at the time, and—"

"Oh, dear. Your hair again?"

"Yes, it snagged on the branches. Lord Hawke was obliged to climb up and untangle me, and I assure you, he wasn't at all pleased about it. Then he accused me of stealing his mistletoe, of all absurd things."

Abby let out a dreamy sigh, as if she hadn't heard a word Helena had just said. "My goodness, Lord Hawke. He's terribly fashionable, you know. Quite the gentleman about town, or so my sister in London says. He's meant to be terribly handsome. How did he look?"

He was a handsome man, certainly, but not a happy one, with that grim cast to his mouth. He did have handsome green eyes, if one overlooked how bloodshot they were. "I don't like to disillusion you, Abby, but he looked dreadful. Like a fox who'd been mauled by a pack of hunting dogs." It wasn't a kind thing to say, but he'd threatened to leave her stuck up the tree, for pity's sake. "He smelled even worse," she added, for good measure.

"*Smelled?*" Abby leapt to her feet, wringing her hands over this distressing detail. "But...but he's an earl!"

Oh, dear. He was, indeed, and her was their employer, too. She cast about for something positive to say, but the only thing he excelled at was cursing. No, wait, there *was* one other thing. "He's an excellent climber. Really, the most accomplished climber, Abby."

But Abby didn't give a fig about climbing. She glanced toward the door, and lowered her voice. "What, ah...what did he smell of?"

"Cheroots, sour brandy, and courtesans. I daresay he came straight from London, from an infamous debauchery. He was missing his hat, his cravat, and one of his boots, too." It was wicked of her to gossip, but she took a perverse delight in the absurd, and a foul-smelling lord was as absurd a thing as they were likely to find in Hawke's Run.

"My goodness. A half-naked, rancid earl!" Abby dropped back onto her chair, overcome. "You have the most extraordinary luck, Miss Templeton."

"Well, he's here now. Perhaps you'll have the

great good fortune to get a whiff of him yourself soon. Until then..." She hesitated, eying her young friend.

Abby was three years younger than she was, and she'd never set foot outside of Hawke's Run, but if anyone could discover the truth behind Lord Hawke's sudden appearance here, it was Abby. For all that she'd never been to London, Abby knew more about what was passing in town than many of the people who lived there.

She had a voracious appetite for scandal, particularly scandal featuring fashionable members of the *ton*, and she was kept well supplied with gossip by her sister Penelope, who had a position as a house-maid in one of the grand London houses.

Helena didn't quite approve of Abby's obsession with title-tattle, but in this case, Abby's knowledge of London's most notorious aristocrats could prove useful. "Lord Hawke looked as if he left London in a hurry, Abby. There must be more to his appearance here this morning than a sudden desire to come home, don't you think?"

"Oh, there's doings afoot, miss, and nothing good, neither. There's a scandal behind it, to be sure. Not Lord Hawke's first, either, but he's such a fa-vorite with the *ton* they tend to forgive him his sins." Abby tapped her lip, thinking. "Still, whatever he's done this time must be awful, indeed, if he's left London."

Helena bit her lip. She didn't like to encourage scandalmongering, but his presence here was certain to agitate the boys. It was rare for a single day to pass without Ryan and Etienne asking after him, and she'd rather know beforehand if he intended to vanish as suddenly as he'd appeared. Surely, that made it an exception? "Will you write to your sister in London, and find out what's behind it?"

"I won't have to." Abby reached around her to grab the teapot, a sly grin on her lips. "If it's as shocking as I suspect, she'll have already written to me. Mark my words, miss. Whatever mischief his lordship's been up to, we'll know what it is before the week is out."

"Thank you, Abby. Now, let's see to the boy's chocolate, shall we? They'll wake soon, and I'd rather they weren't obliged to scamper about searching for me."

She'd learned the hard way the mischief two energetic boys could get into if left to their own devices in an old, empty castle like this one. The last time she'd been late coming to their bedchamber in the morning, she'd been obliged to spend hours searching for them, only to find them teetering atop a dusty ladder in the attic, plucking spiders from the rafters and depositing them in old canning jars so they might "train them up for a spider circus."

"I may as well." Abby let out a theatrical sigh and reached into a cupboard for the block of chocolate. "I suppose preparing the chocolate is the most interesting thing that's ever going to happen to me—"

"Oh, here you are, Miss Templeton." A breathless Mrs. Norris hurried into the kitchen, her wispy gray hair flying about her head. "I'm certain Abby must have told you Lord Hawke has arrived unexpectedly at Hawke's Run this morning. Dear me, I'm rather aflutter, I'm afraid!"

"Yes, she told me, Mrs. Norris, and I saw his lordship coming up the drive." This time, Helena held her tongue about the stench of brandy and courtesans. The less said about *that* the better.

"I've left Lord Hawke in his study," Mrs. Norris said. "He has not yet summoned Ryan and Etienne, and perhaps it would be best, Miss Templeton, if you kept them away from that part of the house until he's prepared to see them. His lordship is rather...fatigued from his journey."

Helena smothered a snort. Fatigued, indeed. Lord Hawke's trouble was that last night's debauchery had caught up to him this morning, and he was as disagreeable as gentlemen generally were under such circumstances.

Mrs. Norris needn't have worried, however, as she'd happily keep the boys as far as possible away from their father, and for as long as she could possibly manage it. It shouldn't prove too difficult. If the past six months were any indication, Lord Hawke had little enough interest in his sons as it was.

It would have been best if he'd kept away, but odds were his lordship would quickly grow bored of the country, and scurry off back to his London amusements before the week was out. "Of course, Mrs. Norris. We'll remain in the schoolroom until luncheon, and then we'll venture outside this afternoon."

Mrs. Norris breathed a sigh of relief. "Very good, Miss Templeton."

"The chocolate is ready, Miss Templeton."

"Thank you, Abby." Helena took the tray with the stout silver chocolate pot and the porcelain cups and strode from the kitchen up the staircase and into the hallway. It was growing rather late. The boys would come in search of her if she didn't appear, and the last thing she wanted was them encountering their bedraggled father on the staircase.

But as soon as she rounded the corner, she heard the unholy clatter of two pairs of six-year-old feet pounding down the staircase. Dash it, she was too late. She hurried forward, the cups rattling on the tray. "Pardon me, my fine gentlemen, but where do you think you're going?"

Two pairs of eyes the same spring green as their father's peered innocently down at her from the first-floor landing. "Our papa's here!" Ryan announced. "We saw him coming up the drive from our bedchamber window."

"He wasn't wearing a hat," Etienne added, as if this bit of information was far too fascinating to wait another minute. "It was *gone!*"

It was, indeed, among other things, most notably his papa's manners. "I see. And has your papa summoned you?"

Adrian, or Ryan, as he was called shook his head. "Not yet, but he—"

"Then you're to march straight back upstairs at once, if you please. You both know the rules. You're to wait in your bedchamber in the mornings until I come fetch you."

"But Miss Templeton—"

"No arguments, if you please. Your father..." Isn't fit to be seen. "Will send for you when he's prepared to see you. Until then, we will proceed as we do every other morning. Up you go."

She braced herself, her fingers tightening around the edges of the tray. For all their high-spirits, Ryan and Etienne were good lads, and she'd made great strides with them since she'd come to Hawke's Run, but they were still little boys, and there were few creatures in all of existence who had less self-control. "Boys," she began in a warning tone. "Did you hear what I—"

But it was already too late. Ryan cast a sidelong glance at Etienne, and then both of them dove toward the bottom of the stairs at once. She leapt to block them—rather a foolish impulse, really, given she was burdened with a heavy tray—but all might still have been well, if Hestia hadn't chosen that moment to make a wild dash for the staircase.

The tiny silver kitten sealed their fate.

She'd become quite nimble over the past six months of chasing two active boys, but the combined pandemonium of Ryan, Etienne and Hestia was too much for any mortal woman.

She stumbled backwards, and a blood-curdling feline shriek split the air as her foot came down hard on poor Hestia's tail. The outraged kitten darted between her feet and up the stairs in a blur of raised gray fur at the same time the boys darted down them. Etienne jumped over a stair in a truly heroic effort to avoid trampling Hestia, but he knocked into his brother, who tumbled down the last two stairs. Etienne landed on top of him, then Helena's feet got tangled in theirs, and she went down, her backside hitting the hard floor with a thud.

As for the tray, it seemed to hang suspended in mid-air for an instant, three horrified pairs of eyes fixed on it until, inevitably, it descended again in a deafening crash of silver and shattered porcelain, the chocolate splattering across the pristine white marble floor in a thick, dark, sticky river.

Helena sat there in the instant of stunned silence

that followed, chocolate dripping off the end of her nose. It was so very dreadful she hardly knew what to do, but Ryan's lips were already wobbling, and Etienne's eyes had filled with tears, and really, there was only one thing one *could* do in such circumstances, wasn't there?

She dissolved into giggles, but soon enough she was gasping with laughter, the sort of great, big belly laughs that drew tears from one's eyes. "Oh dear, this *is* rather a mess, isn't it? Neither of you are hurt, are you, boys?"

They boys shook their heads, dazed still, but little boys were always more apt to laugh than cry, and soon enough uncertain grins were twitching at their lips.

"And you, Hestia? Are you quite alright? I do beg your pardon for stepping on your tail."

Hestia gave a disgruntled meow which set the boys off, and it all might have ended in gales of laughter if it hadn't been for a door slamming open, and a furious voice echoing down the adjacent corridor. "What the *devil* was that ungodly noise?"

Heavy footsteps stomped toward them. Heavy *footstep*, that is, only one boot heel striking the marble, the other lost somewhere between London and Hawke's Run.

The boys gaped at her with wide, anxious eyes. Helena did her best to scramble to her feet, not relishing the idea of facing off with Lord Hawke while sprawled on her backside, but the floor was slippery with chocolate, and she'd only managed to stagger to her knees before his lordship descended upon them, his dark brows drawn so low they looked ready to flee his face altogether.

He looked from her to the boys to the shattered porcelain and flood of chocolate, and his face went as hard as stone. "Explain yourself *this instant*, Miss Templeton."

"It was an accident, my lord. I was going up with the tray, and the boys were coming down, and we collided." Really, what more was there to say? He only had to look to see for himself what had happened. "No one is hurt, thankfully."

"Be that as it may, Miss Templeton," Lord Hawke began, but before he could get another word out, disaster struck.

Well, not disaster so much as Hestia. *Again.*

The kitten, one of a half-dozen from Circe's most recent litter had retreated to a safe corner of the landing, away from the chaos, and was peering down on them through the spaces between the spindles.

That in itself was nothing to fret over. After all, who didn't love kittens? The trouble was that Hestia had a worrying habit of leaping upon the shoulders of unsuspecting passersby, and digging gleefully into their flesh with her claws while they thrashed about trying to dislodge her.

Hestia, likely offended by his shouting, had set her sights on Lord Hawke. Her blue kitten eyes were wide, her tiny behind wriggling as she prepared to leap. "Watch out, my lord—"

But the warning came too late. Hestia was already flying through the air, her front legs extended and claws at the ready, a little bundle of silvery fur and vengeance, and there was Lord Hawke, the flesh of his neck exposed, a perfect target...

Hestia landed on his shoulder, sunk her sharp kitten claws into his neck and held on for dear life, and Lord Hawke let out a bellow that shook the rafters. "What the devil! I've been stung by a bee!"

Oh, dear. That would teach him not to lose his cravat, wouldn't it? Helena scrambled to her feet. "I beg your pardon, my lord! It's not a bee, but a kitten!"

"A kitten? What bloody kitten? There are no cats at Hawke's Run. I detest the things!"

Perhaps there hadn't been six months ago, but there were now, and rather a lot of them. "She doesn't mean any harm, my lord. She's just playful!"

"Her playing is drawing blood! Get this demonic hellcat off me this instant, Miss Templeton!" He whirled around, presenting her with a broad, muscular back.

For a moment she froze, watching in fascination as his muscles flexed under his shirt, but Lord Hawke's thundering voice jerked her back to the emergency at hand. "*Now*, if you don't mind, Miss Templeton!"

"Yes, I—yes, of course." She stumbled around the broken porcelain and caught Hestia by the scruff of her neck, but the kitten clung like a burr as she tugged and scolded, until at last she managed to pry her loose. "Come here, Hestia, you wicked thing."

"Hestia? Does this *creature* belong to you, Miss Templeton?"

"Er...yes?" In truth Hestia and her five brothers and sisters were communal pets, but this didn't seem the right time to delve into the details.

"Your *pet*, Miss Templeton." Lord Hawke pointed an accusing finger at the kitten. "Has just destroyed a costly linen shirt, and that's to say nothing of a silk waistcoat with hand-carved mother-of-pearl buttons!"

Helena clutched Hestia closer to protect her from his stabbing finger. "Nonsense. It was already spoiled when you rode up the drive. It's hardly fair to blame Hestia for your own carelessness."

Oh, *no*. Perhaps she shouldn't have said that. His face was turning an alarming shade of red.

Lord Hawke drew himself up to his full height, which was impressive, indeed, though the effect was rather dampened by the droplets of bright red blood staining the neck of his shirt. "Pack your things, Miss Templeton. Your services at Hawke's Run are no longer required."

THREE

Miss Templeton gaped up at him, the demonic hellcat who'd sliced the back of his neck into ribbons clutched to her breast. "You're dismissing me because of a *cat*?"

She was doused in drinking chocolate with shattered bits of porcelain tangled in the hems of her skirts, and she thought this was about the *cat*? Was the woman mad, or merely dull-witted?

But the cat hadn't helped matters. There was only one circumstance under which a man appreciated claws in his back, and this was *not* it. He eyed the furry gray menace, who was still glaring at him from the safety of Miss Templeton's arms. "I'm dismissing you, Miss Templeton, because it's obvious to me you aren't suited to act as governess for two energetic young boys."

For one glorious moment she was rendered speechless, but she regained the power of her tongue before he had a chance to relish it. "May I ask, Lord Hawke, how you came to the conclusion that I can't properly care for your sons?"

How? Surely, that must be obvious? "I arrived

home less than two hours ago, Miss Templeton. In that time, you've abused my tree, reduced my porcelain to a powder, and now you're sprawled at the bottom of my staircase in a puddle of drinking chocolate. Are you somehow under the impression you've presented yourself favorably? On the contrary, it's abundantly clear to me you aren't proper for this post."

Though to her credit, she *had* lasted much longer than the six previous governesses who'd held it prior to her arrival. His boys were high-spirited, or perhaps boisterous was a better word, or...oh, for God's sake, very well, then. They were rowdy, wild imps, their natural exuberance gone feral from a succession of spineless governesses who let them do as they pleased.

"Not qualified!" Her brows lowered, and her eyes darkened with such fury for a moment he thought she'd hurl her attack kitten at his head. "I beg your pardon, my lord, but as you said, you've only just returned home. I grant you we've had a few, er...unfortunate mishaps this morning, but it hardly seems fair for you to assess my fitness as governess based on those events alone."

He didn't give a bloody damn whether it was fair or not. He was the *earl*, and he didn't need any reason at all to dismiss her. "I think it's perfectly fair, Miss Templeton, and as I'm the earl, my opinion is the only one that matters."

Angry color surged into her cheeks. "And your sons, Lord Hawke? What of them? Does their welfare matter? Are their best interests of any concern to you at all, or—"

"You needn't trouble yourself with my sons' welfare any longer, Miss Templeton. I assure you they'll be properly cared for. My decision is final. Once you've gathered your things, a servant will take you to Steeple Barton to catch the mail coach."

She raised her chin with far more dignity than a lady who'd fallen on her arse had any right to command, shook the loose bits of porcelain from her skirts, and offered him a glare that could have drawn blood from a stone. "You're making a mistake, Lord Hawke, but I can see it's pointless to argue with you. I'll be ready to leave within the—"

"*Noooo!*"

The shout came from Etienne, spilling from his lips like a thunderclap. It bounced off the timbered ceilings and hit Adrian's eardrums with the force of a blow. "God in heaven, Etienne! What—"

"*No, no, no!*" Etienne had clambered to his feet and was standing at the bottom of the stairs, his arms rigid at his sides and his small body shaking, his head thrown back and a howl of pure fury on his lips. "No!"

Adrian stared at the boy, shocked. "Etienne, what the devil is the—"

"I don't *want* Miss Templeton to go away!" Etienne's face was scarlet, tears streaming down his cheeks. "You can't make her go!"

"We'll discuss it later, Etienne, after—"

He was cut off by a deafening crash, and whirled around to find his namesake and heir had snatched up the silver chocolate pot and hurled it at the wall with all the strength in his six-year-old body. The dented pot hit the floor and tumbled down the last few steps, chocolate dripping from the spout.

Ryan dove for one of the larger bits of broken porcelain, no doubt intending to send it the way of the chocolate pot, but Adrian shot forward, stumbling over the mess on the floor, and seized Ryan around his middle before he could cut his hands on the sharp edges. "No, Ryan! Don't touch that!" He held the boy's arms to his side. "Stop this at once!"

But Ryan was well past the point of stopping. He raged like a wild thing, heaving and thrashing in Adrian's arms, kicking his legs and twisting like an eel in his effort to be free. "No! Let me go! I don't want *you*, I want Miss Templeton, and now you're sending her away, and we'll be all alone again!"

Adrian stared down at his son's red, twisted face, frozen with shock. Never before, not *once* had his boys shown the least loyalty to any of their previous governesses. On the contrary, they'd driven them off one after the next with their mad antics, but now they were ready to tear the house apart in defense of Miss Templeton?

He whirled around to face her, but she didn't spare him a glance. She'd taken Etienne into her arms and was murmuring to him, smoothing his hair as he sobbed against her shoulder.

"Let me go!" Ryan screamed. "You're *never* home, and now you've come and ruined *everything*! I hate—"

"That's enough, Ryan." Miss Templeton's calm voice cut through Ryan's hysterical shrieking. "I know you're very angry right now, but you may not speak to your father that way. Now, take a deep breath, and beg his pardon."

Adrian waited for another shriek of fury in response to this command, but somehow Miss Templeton's quiet voice pierced the bubble of Ryan's frenzy, and all the fight drained out of him. His body went limp, his thin shoulders sagging. "I'm sorry, papa," he mumbled, wiping an arm over his eyes.

"I...it's..." What? He hadn't the vaguest idea what to say, or how to make sense of what had just happened, so he said only, "Miss Templeton, I would appreciate it if you would take the boys upstairs to their bedchamber."

She cast him a flinty look, but she did as he bid her, taking each of the boys' hands in hers and disappearing up the stairs without a word.

He turned on his heel, strode to his study and closed the door behind him.

What had just happened?

He was shaking as he reached for the crystal decanter and glass Mrs. Norris had left on the sideboard, poured himself a measure of brandy, then dropped into the chair behind his desk and let his head fall into his hands.

Pain throbbed in his temples, his eyeballs were sticky with grit, he needed a bath in the worst way, and there was hardly enough brandy left in the decanter to get him through the rest of the morning.

And his boys. His boys despised him.

Of course, they did. Had he expected anything less, after he'd kept away from Hawke's Run for so long? Hadn't there been a part of him who'd *wanted* this to happen? A secret, shameful part that believed it would be easier for them if they no longer expected anything of him?

Easier for them, or easier for you?

It was Sophie's voice in his head. He was too much of a coward to ask such an honest question of himself, but she'd never been one to flatter him, or tell him pretty lies. She'd always told the truth, no matter how difficult it was to say, or how painful to hear.

He'd loved that about her, had always admired her honesty and bravery, but somehow in the two agonizing years since her death he'd grown accustomed to lying to himself again.

If she could see what a bloody mess he'd made of things, she'd be raining curses down on him from the heavens even now. Yes, indeed, he'd done a tidy bit of work for one morning, hadn't he? Shouting, shrieking and tears were just what one wished for their homecoming.

He'd only just arrived, and he'd already tipped the entire house over into chaos. It would have been better for all of them if he'd remained in London and weathered the storm of this latest scandal alone rather than drawing his sons into it with his ill-conceived return this morning.

This was all Lady Pamela's bloody fault, for tangling him up in her ridiculous schemes. He hadn't even done anything wrong this time, for God's sake. He was perfectly innocent of the crimes the gossips were insisting he'd committed, but it hardly mattered.

He'd been guilty too many times before.

If it wasn't for Lady Pamela's antics, he might have gone on as he had been, drinking the memories away and lying to himself, but it was too late now. He was here, for better or worse—

Worse. Certainly worse. Surely, they could all agree on that?

Mrs. Norris was going to be furious when she discovered he'd dismissed Miss Templeton. She'd be obliged to manage the boys until another governess could be found. Perhaps one of the village girls might be persuaded to take them on until—

"Lord Hawke!" There was a sharp knock on his study door, and Mrs. Norris's voice came from the other side. "I beg your pardon, my lord, but might I have a word?"

He tossed back the rest of his brandy and wiped his mouth with his soiled sleeve. He may as well have it out with his housekeeper now. It wasn't as if this morning could get any worse. "Come in, Mrs. Norris."

The door opened, and she marched inside. "I understand you've dismissed Miss Templeton, my lord."

Well, that news hadn't taken long to make its way to his housekeeper. "Yes, that's correct, Mrs. Norris. Miss Templeton is not a suitable governess for—"

"You've made a dreadful mistake, Lord Hawke, and must rectify it at once."

He gaped at her. Mrs. Norris had been the housekeeper at Hawke's Run for more than two decades, and in that time, she'd never ventured to question his judgment, much less presume to issue him a command. "I beg your pardon, but I haven't the least intention of doing any such thing."

"You must, my lord. Please, call her back down at once. Tell her you've changed your mind, and beg her to stay."

Beg Miss Templeton? It would be a frosty day in hell before he'd beg her for a single thing. "Certainly not. It's quite out of the ques—"

"If Miss Templeton leaves this house, Lord Hawke, then I will follow her right out the door."

"*What?*" For God's sake, had Miss Templeton bewitched them all? "You can't mean that, Mrs. Norris!"

"Indeed, I do, and if I leave, I daresay Abby will be right on my heels."

"Abby?" Who the devil was Abby?

"Abigail Hurley, my lord. Your kitchen maid."

"Never heard of her."

Mrs. Norris huffed. "She's been with us for nearly a year, my lord. If you recall, last year you gave me leave to hire whatever servants I deemed necessary to efficiently run your household."

Had he, indeed? He had no memory of that, but then he'd rarely passed a sober day in London since he'd fled Hawke's Run all those months ago.

"I chose both Abby and Mrs. Templeton after much judicious consideration," Mrs. Norris went on, "and I have never had cause to regret either—"

"Did you happen to see the remnants of this morning's catastrophe at the bottom of the staircase when you passed, Mrs. Norris? I would think that alone was enough cause for regret."

"It was an accident, my lord. Surely, you don't blame Miss Templeton for an accident that might have happened to anyone?"

"I don't *blame* her, Mrs. Norris." Of course, he blamed her. Whose fault was it, if not hers? "But surely you see that Miss Templeton is a small little bit of a thing, and not physically up to the task of managing two energetic young boys. She also happens to be a single young lady."

A rather attractive single young lady, at that. Those eyes...

He cleared his throat. "It's not appropriate for her to remain here, now I've returned to Hawke's Run." If he'd been any less of an infamous rake it might not have mattered, but here they were.

34

"Governesses do tend to be single ladies, my lord, and there's nothing scandalous about it, but if you're concerned for Miss Templeton's reputation, I will personally take responsibility for her well-being while she remains under your roof."

He drummed his fingers against his desk, eying her. "I don't understand, Mrs. Norris. At least half a dozen governesses and as many nursemaids have come and gone from Hawke's Run since..."

Since Sophie died.

But he wouldn't think on that just now. The memories would catch him soon enough, just as they always did when he was here. "Are you so reluctant to take on Ryan and Etienne until another governess can be found? I'm aware they're rather a handful—"

"That isn't it at all, my lord. I love those boys as if they were my own, as naughty as they are. That's the very reason why I can't stand by silently by while you dismiss Miss Templeton. She's turned Ryan and Etienne around, and make no mistake. You won't find another like her, and it isn't...forgive me, Lord Hawke, but it isn't fair to the boys to take her away from them when they have so little constancy in their lives."

He winced. Well, that was plain enough.

He'd never intended to stay away from Hawke's Run as long as he had. Business had taken him to London, but once he was there, he'd lost himself in an endless round of drinking and debauchery. Every morning over the past six months he'd woken with an aching head and bleary eyes and sworn to himself he'd return home to his sons that very day, but then the numbing cycle would begin again, and he'd lose another day.

And another, and another...

Now he was home, and his boys had grown so much like Sophie that looking into their eyes was like looking through a window into the past. Or was it a looking glass? Yes, a shattered looking glass, with the reflection of the life that should have been theirs, only with a massive crack down the middle that distorted everything, ruined it—

"...she has a way with the boys I've never seen before, and as you're aware, my lord, Ryan and Etienne become more wild, more unruly with every subsequent governess."

It was his fault his boys were so lost. Their every struggle, their every failing—all of it was his fault. He couldn't bear to scold them, or lecture them, or shout at them.

He couldn't bear to look at them...

He loved them desperately, but with a strange sort of fierce hopelessness, forever torn between the urge to snatch them both tightly to him, and push them away for their own good. He might have become a decent father with Sophie's help, but she was gone, and bit by bit he'd fallen back into the same disgraceful behavior he'd indulged in before he'd made her his.

He was, alas, his father's son. If that weren't bad enough, he was also his sons' father, and his boys deserved so much more, so much better than him—

"...a truly extraordinary talent with children."

He dragged his attention back to Mrs. Norris, who was still talking. She was a dry woman, not given to extravagant praise, but she was waxing veritably poetic about Miss Templeton. "I don't know how she manages it, but they adore and respect her in equal measure. Indeed, my lord she's done wonders with them. They want to please her, and hang on her every word."

That little bit of a blue-eyed thing and her fiendish hell cat had tamed his wild boys? Surely not, yet to hear Mrs. Norris tell it, Miss Templeton was the patron saint of wicked children.

"Indeed, my lord, you do Ryan and Etienne great injury, dismissing Miss Templeton. I simply cannot let it happen without voicing how strenuously I object to—"

"Yes, yes, all right, Mrs. Norris." He held up his hand to quiet her. "I'll have a word with Miss Templeton. But I make no promises. If I find she's lacking the qualifications to properly instruct my boys, then I *will* dismiss her."

"I'm certain you'll find her qualifications more than adequate, my lord."

Doubtful. How much knowledge could the girl possibly have? She couldn't be more than nineteen or twenty years old. "That remains to be seen."

"Yes, my lord, and thank you, my lord. I assure you that you won't regret it."

"That remains to be seen, as well," he muttered, pouring himself another measure of brandy, because clearly the trouble *wasn't* that he'd had too much brandy last night, but that he hadn't had enough of it yet today. "Please tell her I wish to see her at once."

"Right away, Lord Hawke."

Mrs. Norris hurried out the door, and he slumped in his chair, his glass clutched in his hand. He'd told Miss Templeton her dismissal was final, and she didn't seem like the forgetful sort, so he'd likely be swallowing a healthy draught of his pride along with the brandy soon enough.

A few minutes later, there was a sharp rap, and he looked up from his morose study of his glass to find Miss Templeton standing in the open doorway.

Even her knock was impertinent.

"Mrs. Norris bid me come and see you, my lord."

"Yes. Come in, Miss Templeton, and close the door behind you, if you would." He eyed her as she pushed the door closed and approached him. She hadn't yet changed out of her ruined gown, and a strong smell of chocolate wafted around her, the thick, rich scent of it threatening to make him gag.

"Sit down." He nodded at the chair in front of his desk. "Mrs. Norris is of the opinion that I've made a mistake, dismissing you."

One dark eye brow rose. "Oh?"

Good Lord, but that was a damning eyebrow. "Yes, ah, she seems to think you're good for the boys, and her opinion is not one I readily dismiss."

Nothing. No reply, or change in her expression. She simply stared at him with those cool, gray blue eyes, and she looked as if she could keep it up for a good long while, too.

"I, ah...I'm willing to give you another chance, Miss Templeton, if you promise to take more care in the future."

Still, she said nothing, merely waited, her hands folded neatly in her lap.

Damn the woman, she was going to make him grovel.

He supposed he'd do the same, in her position. "Will you please consent to stay on as governess at Hawke's Run, Miss Templeton? The boys seem fond of you, and I'd rather not disrupt their lives with a search for a new governess."

"*Stay*, my lord?" She rested a hand on her chest, her eyes wide. "But what of your poor trees, and your shattered porcelain? Are you certain you're willing to risk it all by keeping me on? And that's to say nothing of your mother-of-pearl buttons!"

He pointed a finger at her. "Never mind the blasted buttons, but my dislike of that wretched cat of yours is perfectly justified. That creature tore a gash as long as my forearm into my neck. I would have fared better against a guillotine!"

Her eyes narrowed. "If I stay, Lord Hawke, then Hestia stays with me."

Good Lord, but swallowing one's pride was a foul, bitter business, wasn't it? "Yes, alright. The murderous little fiend can stay, too, but keep her out of my way. Do you agree to remain at Hawke's Run, then?"

Once again, she fell silent.

Was she really going to refuse him, just to deal him the set-down he deserved?

The answer to that question was destined to forever remain a mystery, because just as she opened her mouth to reply, there was a pitiful little sniff from the other side of the closed door, followed by a stifled sob, and a mournful, "Oh, *please*, Miss Templeton! Please don't go!"

With that, Miss Templeton's fate was sealed, and his right along with it.

"Very well, my lord. I'll stay." She grinned as a whoop came from the other side of the door. She had a fetching smile. A fetching mouth, come to that, full and plump and—

Never mind her mouth.

"Your charges await, Miss Templeton." He waved

a hand toward the door, desperate to be rid of her. "You may go, and close the door behind you."

"As you wish, my lord."

She rose to her feet, and offered him a curtsy that somehow managed to be impertinent rather than deferential. Rather a neat trick, that.

Once she was gone, he swallowed the last of the brandy in his glass and sagged back against his chair. God above, what a morning. He'd lost and then re-gained both a housekeeper and a governess, and evidently gained a kitchen maid named Abby, a chit he'd never before laid eyes on, and wouldn't know if he stumbled over her...

When he woke up sometime later, the mantel clock was chiming, the brandy he'd drunk was burning a hole in his belly, and it suddenly occurred to him he'd let Miss Templeton escape his study without asking for her academic qualifications.

He glanced at the clock, and let out a groan.

It wasn't even eleven o'clock in the morning yet.

CHAPTER
FOUR

Hestia spent the night in Helena's bedchamber hunting imaginary rodents, scampering up and down the silk draperies and nibbling on the ends of Helena's hair. It didn't make for a restful night, and she woke bleary-eyed and groggy the following morning.

The kitten was a great nuisance, but after yesterday's fiasco on the staircase, she'd just as soon keep Hestia out of Lord Hawke's sight in case he flew into another temper and tossed her out the door.

Not *just* Hestia, but herself, as well.

No doubt it would grow tiresome, having to tiptoe about the castle and duck around corners like some sort of thief, but whatever scandal had chased Lord Hawke from London would be forgotten soon enough. The *ton*'s outrage would vanish the instant another scandal caught their attention, and he'd be on his way back to town before Mrs. Norris was obliged to replenish the brandy in the crystal decanter in his study.

Or nearly so. Brandy seemed to be one of the few things Lord Hawke did approve of.

The difficulty would come once he was gone, as Ryan and Etienne were sure to be devastated. Tears, anger and questions with no answers would follow, but she'd deal with that once it happened. At the moment, she'd have her hands full keeping away from Lord Hawke, as he was certain to dismiss her for good if there was another confrontation between them.

"Good morning, Miss Templeton," Abby called as she entered the kitchen, but the cheerful smile fell from her lips when Helena collapsed at the table with a groan. "Oh, dear. You don't look well at all. Are you ill?"

"No, just fatigued. Hestia isn't the most decorous of bedmates, I'm afraid."

"No, I don't imagine she is. Can't you put her out?"

"It's best if she stays in my bedchamber while Lord Hawke's here." Helena accepted the cup of tea Abby offered her with a grateful smile. "He doesn't like cats, not even kittens."

Abby snorted. "That's not the only thing he doesn't like, from what I hear. He's a bit hard to please, by all accounts."

"He's not overly fond of governesses, if that's what you mean." Or mistletoe. Or trees, morning sunshine, and drinking chocolate. At this point it would be easier to list the things Lord Hawke *did* approve of, rather than those that threw him into a temper.

"Bad luck, miss, that mishap on the stairs yesterday. I'll carry the boys' tray up this morning, if you like."

"You're a good soul, Abby, but there's no need. The boys are on their way down already. We have our animal husbandry lesson in the stables this morning, and will take our chocolate in the kitchen afterwards."

"Alright then, miss. But speaking of animals, what will you do about the rest of the kittens? They're scattered all about the castle, you know, and one or the other of them is sure to cross Lord Hawke's path sooner or later."

"Yes, I thought of that." Helena set her teacup down with a sigh. "I'm afraid there's not much I can do but gather as many of them as I can find and put them in my bedchamber until Lord Hawke is gone."

"What, all of them, miss? But you'll not get another wink of sleep with those little imps scampering about!"

"Perhaps they'll keep each other entertained, and leave me out of it." But of course, that wouldn't happen. It was pure self-delusion to imagine a half-dozen kittens could somehow prove to be less troublesome than one, but as far as Lord Hawke was aware, Hestia was the only cat on the premises, and it was best to keep it that way. "Have you heard anything from Lord Hawke yet this morning? He hasn't ventured from his bedchamber yet, has he?"

"Oh no, miss. I doubt you'll have to worry about him for some time. Fashionable sorts like Lord Hawke never rise before late in the afternoon, you know. I daresay we won't see hide nor hair of him before teatime."

"My goodness, Abby, you're right! I didn't even think of that." That was good news! It reduced her chances of running into him quite significantly, didn't it? It was just the reprieve she needed to lift her spirits. "Why, with a little luck, I'll hardly have to see him at all."

"One hopes not, miss."

Indeed, now she thought of it, even when he was awake, he wasn't likely to stir a step much beyond his bedchamber and study. It was all going to be just fine, and she was a perfect goose, worrying herself into a tizzy as she'd done. "I'd best be off. I daresay the boys are waiting for me. Thank you for the tea, Abby."

She waved to her friend, then hurried up the stairs, a spring in her step, a smile rising to her lips when she saw Etienne and Ryan already in the entryway. "Good morning, boys. My, you're both prompt this morning. Are you ready for our lesson?"

"No." Ryan shook his head, his gaze on the staircase. "Our papa isn't here yet."

"Your papa?" Oh, no. Did the boys think their father was going to rise this early in the morning and join them in their lessons? Where could they have gotten such an idea? Now she was going to have to explain that he wasn't coming, and their tender little hearts were going to be broken.

She knelt down in front of them and put a hand on each thin shoulder. "I'm sorry, boys, but I don't think your papa will be able—"

"Good morning, Miss Templeton."

The deep voice coming from behind her so startled her she nearly fell flat on her face, but she managed to stumble to her feet, and there, at the top of the stairs was Lord Hawke, peering down upon her like a king reviewing his lowly subjects.

He *wasn't* still asleep. He wasn't in bed at all, or even in his bedchamber as he should be, but at the top of the stairs, his brows lowered in the same fearsome scowl he'd worn when he'd found her at the bottom of the stairs yesterday morning, half-drowned in drinking chocolate.

It was becoming distressingly familiar, the scowl.

"My sons tell me we're to have our morning lesson in the stables, Miss Templeton," Lord Hawke said, making his way down the stairs.

He looked nearly as disheveled as he'd been when he appeared in the drive yesterday, his clothing askew and his dark hair matted with sweat. He was no longer filthy—he'd had a bath, thankfully, and the stench of debauchery was no longer clinging to him —but it didn't look as if he'd passed a restful evening.

His complexion was gray, his eyes ringed with dark circles, and thin lines of exhaustion were etched into the corners of his mouth. Even so, there was a strong resemblance between him and his sons, particularly his eyes, which were the dark green of forest ferns.

"I fail to see why you're dragging us outdoors in this freezing weather." He paused at the bottom of the stairs and frowned down at her with his arms crossed over his wide chest. "Is the schoolroom not sufficient for your purposes?"

A sharp retort rose to her lips, and it was a harder struggle than it should have been for her to bite it back. It wasn't fair, dash it. He was meant to be in his bed for hours yet, or in his study drinking brandy, or on his way back to London—anywhere but *here*, tormenting her.

"Good morning, my lord," she managed through gritted teeth. "It is rather cold, I grant you, but this morning's lesson is—"

"It's animal husbands, papa." Etienne beamed at

his father. "Animal husbands is always in the stables."

Lord Hawke's dark brows went from lowered to imperiously arched in the blink of an eye. Really, the man had the most judgmental eyebrows. "Animal husbands, Miss Templeton? Is that some new course of study I'm not familiar with?"

"Etienne means animal husbandry, my lord."

"Animal husbandry? How curious. Tell me, Miss Templeton, how is it you're teaching the boys animal husbandry when there's not a single livestock animal to be found anywhere on the property?"

No, there wasn't, and it was shameful, as any gentleman with as substantial a property as Hawke's Run should have a basic knowledge of livestock and agriculture. And yes, perhaps 'animal husbandry' was a bit too grand a title for their lessons, but what harm was there in that? "We make do with what we have, my lord."

"Animal husbands is good fun, papa. You'll see." Ryan took Lord Hawke's hand, his sweet young face bright and open as he gazed up at his father, yesterday's fury and disappointment quickly forgotten, as was always the way with little boys.

No one was more forgiving than a child.

Right up until the point where they'd been disappointed one time too many times, and then nothing —not pleas, tears or the bitterest regrets—would ever persuade them to forgive again.

How many more chances did Lord Hawke have?

It wasn't a question she could answer, or even one she should ask, as it wasn't her concern. Anyway, it didn't matter today, because he was here now, Etienne's and Ryan's small hands tucked into his larger ones.

The boys were so pleased and proud, skipping along at their father's side as they made their way down the pathway that led to the stables, frosty clouds of air spilling from their lips as they chattered to him about the horse he'd ridden from London, which was tucked safely into a stall in the stables.

Guilt crept over her as she took in their happy faces. It was dreadful of her to wish Lord Hawke away from Hawke's Run when the boys were so starved for his attention. He'd be gone soon enough, leaving them confused and disappointed, but at least they'd have this brief time with him. Later, perhaps they'd recall this tiny sliver of a memory of him being home, and spending a few fleeting moments with them. Perhaps that would make it worth all the heartache it would cause them when he disappeared again—

"Did you grow up on a farm, Miss Templeton?"

She turned, startled to find the boys had run ahead to the stables, and Lord Hawke had come up alongside her. "No, my lord, but on an estate rather like this one, though not so grand as this. My father was far more interested in plants than animal farming, and we didn't keep a stable."

"I see. Then how are you qualified to teach the boys animal husbandry?"

"Are you enquiring into my qualifications, Lord Hawke?" *Now*, six months after she'd become his sons' governess?

He gave her a thin smile. "You look surprised, Miss Templeton, but Ryan will become the Earl of Hawke one day, and Etienne a gentleman of consequence by virtue of the family's title and fortune alone. You can't suppose I would leave their education to chance."

Why shouldn't she suppose so? He'd left every other aspect of their lives to chance. It hardly made sense he'd trouble himself about their education. This waspish reply leapt to her lips, but she wrestled it back down her throat. It wouldn't do her any good at all to bait Lord Hawke. She could hold her tongue, for Ryan and Etienne's sake. "Of course not, my lord. As to my qualifications—"

"In addition to animal husbandry, I assume you teach mathematics, history, geography and literature, as well as Latin, Greek and French. I trust you're knowledgeable in all the physical, earth and life sciences, and philosophy, as well?"

My, he certainly sounded skeptical. "Our mutual friend Lady Fosberry arranged with Mrs. Norris for me to apply for this position, Lord Hawke. Do you suppose she would have recommended me as governess if I can't tell Shakespeare from Marlowe, or Copernicus from Newton?"

"That isn't an answer. I'm waiting, Miss Templeton."

She stared at him, the thread of control she had over her temper threatening to snap again. That was *precisely* what he thought. He'd decided, in spite of Lady Fosberry's recommendation, that she wasn't qualified to teach his sons! Her hackles rose until every inch of her was tingling with indignation.

"Very well, my lord. I teach Latin, Greek, French, Italian and German." She counted them off on her fingers. "I'm perfectly well versed in literature, philosophy and mathematics, but aside from a fondness for Greek mythology, I prefer the sciences. I teach anatomy, chemistry, physics and astronomy, although I prefer the biological sciences. Zoology and botany are particular favorites of mine."

"Botany? Bravo, Miss Templeton. You're as knowledgeable as any Oxford don, then."

Her teeth snapped together. "I never claimed to be anything of the sort, but neither have I exaggerated or embellished upon my qualifications. I have no need to."

"Be that as it may, leafing through a few books in your family's library hardly qualifies you to teach the sons of an earl botany, anatomy and animal husbandry. May I assume you're self-taught, Miss Templeton?"

"I don't care much for assumptions, Lord Hawke. I find they're generally wrong."

"I see. Then you're not self-taught?"

"No, I'm not. My father taught me. Are you familiar with the name James Templeton, Lord Hawke?"

"James Templeton? It sounds vaguely familiar."

"He was rather well known in Royal Society circles as one of London's most brilliant scholars, particularly in the field of botany. James Templeton is—was—my father."

"I can't say I spend a great deal of my time in London with members of the Royal Society, Miss Templeton."

She smothered a snort. *That* wasn't difficult to believe. Perhaps if she'd mentioned the name of one of London's most celebrated Cyprians, then he might have had more luck. "When my father was alive, he took it upon himself to educate me and my sisters. If you would have considered James Templeton a proper tutor for your sons, my lord, then you can have no quibble with me as their governess."

"I'm merely enquiring, Miss Templeton. I never said I had any quibble with your—"

"Shall we catch up to the boys, Lord Hawke? They've just disappeared into the stables, and I prefer to be there when they're near the animals." She didn't wait for an answer, but hurried off toward the stables, her head high.

He could follow her, or return to the castle on his own, just as he wished, but either way, she was quite finished answering Lord Hawke's questions.

She was a reasonable person. A kind one, even, and not quick to anger, but as any of her sisters would attest, she could be unpleasant indeed when her temper was stirred.

And Lord Hawke was coming dangerously close to pushing her too far.

CHAPTER
FIVE

Miss Templeton marched off toward the stables, her head high, chin up, and the slender line of her back rigid with irritation, leaving Adrian slack-jawed in her wake.

What did the woman *mean*, interrupting him while he was speaking, then stomping off without so much as a backward glance? She was awfully haughty for a governess, lecturing him about anatomy and botany and the danger of making assumptions, all with that glimmer of temper in her eyes.

Yes, she was entirely too high in the instep for a servant, though to be fair, he may have been a trifle hostile just now. No doubt that had set her teeth on edge. Damned if he knew what it was about her that turned him into such an insufferable arse, but something about her forthright gaze doused the charm he was so admired for in London.

In certain circles, at any rate.

He glanced between the castle and the open stable door. If he had any sense at all he'd go back to his bed and leave his uppity governess to conduct her lesson in peace. It was bloody freezing out here, so cold his fingers had gone numb, and he'd left a blazing fire in his bedchamber.

Yet as much as he detested the idea of running after Miss Templeton like some naughty schoolboy, he couldn't quite make his feet turn back toward the castle. It wouldn't do for her to think she'd chased him off. No, that would give her far too much satisfaction, and then there was the matter of these mysterious animal husbandry lessons.

Who were these animals they were studying? Miss Templeton had said they 'made do with what they had,' which was suspicious in itself. At the moment, the stables housed only Cyrus, the horse he'd ridden from London, and a few old cart horses. There were no cows to milk, no pigs to slaughter, not even any chickens, and hence, no eggs. How could Miss Templeton be conducting animal husbandry lessons without any animals about?

Surely, he should know what was going on in his own stables? He was the earl, after all.

He picked his way across the stable-yard, skirting a pile of frozen horse dung and ducked inside the stables, blinking in the dim light and breathing in the familiar scents of dust and hay, and underlying that, faint but unmistakable, the earthy, animal smell of what had once been a busy stable with dozens of horses and servants bustling about. Had that only been three years ago? It seemed like another lifetime, when he and Sophie used to rise early in the mornings so they might ride out together.

But the stables were empty now, aside from Cyrus, who was tucked into a stall busily munching his hay. The horse lifted his head when Adrian entered and stuck his nose over his stall door with a whinny of welcome.

"Hello, boy." He gave the horse's nose an absent stroke, but his attention was caught by Miss Templeton, Ryan and Etienne, who were crouched over something in a far corner of the stables, their heads bent together. Miss Templeton was murmuring something to them, her voice too low for him to hear her, so he crept closer, and saw the edge of a wooden pen.

"...startle her, Etienne, and be careful of her claws. She's still quite wild, you know, and her claws are very sharp. You won't like it if she scratches you."

Good Lord, did he even want to know what she had in that pen? Not raccoons, surely? Or, God forbid, rats? Surely even Miss Templeton would draw the line at rats?

He drew closer, peering over their shoulders, and saw...not rats. Whatever was in the pen was too big to be a rat, thankfully, because the only thing he despised more than rats was—

"Her belly is very fat," Ryan was leaning so far over the side of the pen he was in danger of toppling in. "When is she going to have her babies, Miss Templeton?"

"Let's consult the chart, shall we?" Miss Templeton drew a neatly folded paper from the pocket of her cloak. "Now, we know domestic cats gestate for sixty-four to seventy-one days, and most commonly deliver between days sixty-three and sixty-five. Now, boys, according to the chart, how long has Hecate here been—"

"*Cats*? For God's sake, Miss Templeton, you call *this* animal husbandry?"

The three heads hanging over the side of the pen all jerked around at once. Etienne and Ryan's eyes went wide, but Miss Templeton's narrowed, and she rose to her feet, dusting the hay from her skirts. "Is something wrong, Lord Hawke?"

"*Wrong*? Of course, there is. It's no wonder my house is overrun with cats! You're breeding them in my stables!"

"Breeding them? I beg your pardon, Lord Hawke, but you *are* familiar with the habits of stable cats, are you not? I've no need to breed them. They take care of that themselves."

Unbelievably, a hint of a smile touched her lips. A smile, of all infuriating things, as if she found his objections amusing. "I believe I've made it perfectly clear that I despise cats, Miss Templeton."

One dark eyebrow rose. "Abundantly so, yes, but this isn't about *you*, my lord."

"Hecate is a *good* cat, papa." Ryan scrambled to his feet. "She's not naughty like Hestia. She's never leapt on us, or bitten or scratched us."

"She doesn't come inside the house, papa." Etienne twisted his hands together. "She likes living in her pen."

"Forgive me, Lord Hawke, but I'm afraid I don't see what all the fuss is about. Surely, there's no harm in observing the gestational calendar of domestic cats for educational purposes—"

"There's nothing educational about observing feral cats, Miss Templeton, no matter if you do present it under the guise of teaching the boys animal husbandry."

Silence, then one word, hard and clipped. "Guise?"

"Hecate's going to have her babies very soon, papa." Etienne's anxious gaze was moving between Adrian and Miss Templeton. "You can't send her off now. What will she do?"

"You needn't worry, Etienne." Miss Templeton's cool gaze never left Adrian's face. "No one is going to send Hecate off, I promise you."

It hadn't even occurred to him to get rid of the cat, but whatever wicked impulse had been urging him to bedevil Miss Templeton since the moment he'd laid eyes on her made him snap, "That isn't up to you, Miss Templeton. You have no business promising anyone anything."

It was, once again, the perfectly wrong thing to say.

Etienne let out a little cry and hopped over the side of Hecate's pen, throwing his small body in front of the cat as if to protect her, and Ryan moved in front of his brother, his hand up to keep Adrian back. "You can't take her away, papa. We won't let you."

"Take her away?" He stared at his boys in astonishment. Did they truly think he'd do away with their cat? "I'm not going to *take* her—"

"It's alright, boys. Hecate isn't going anywhere."

Miss Templeton's voice had gone so soft it was hardly above a whisper, but something about it made him pause. God knew he hadn't the vaguest idea how to read her, but that shift in tone and the flush of color streaking her cheekbones were, in his experience, universal to all females.

They meant he'd do well to hold his tongue.

But it was too late for that. Miss Templeton's eyes had narrowed to blueish gray slits. "Is it your intention, Lord Hawke, to interfere with all of my lessons?"

"I...no, of course not. I simply mean to point out that animal husbandry is a science concerned with *livestock*. Since when are cats considered livestock?"

"Do you see any livestock here, Lord Hawke?" She swept an arm around the stables.

"Well, no, but that's——"

"As I'm sure you're aware, my lord, animal husbandry is a varied science, with many different elements of animal management and agriculture. I'd prefer livestock for my lessons, of course, but the boys will learn a great deal, regardless of the species of animal. Wouldn't you agree, Lord Hawke?"

"I don't see that there's much to learn from cats, but——"

"Might I have a word with you, my lord?" She didn't pause for an answer, but marched to the other end of the stables and stood there with her arms crossed over her chest, foot tapping as she waited.

A refusal didn't seem likely to help matters at this point, so he followed reluctantly after her, feeling every inch a wicked schoolboy on his way to a sound thrashing. "I beg your pardon, Miss Templeton, but I——"

"Is it your intention, Lord Hawke, to take Hecate away from Ryan and Etienne?"

"What? No, of course not. I'm not fond of cats, but I'd never take their——"

"You're aware, are you not, my lord, that your sons think you're about to do just that?"

No, they couldn't possibly think he'd do something so cruel as that.

Could they? "No, they don't. They know I'd never——"

"They don't know anything of the sort." She

nodded toward the other end of the stables. "Look at them, my lord. Anyone can see you've upset them."

He did as she bid him, and his heart sank. The boys were still standing in front of the pen, their small bodies tense and their wary gazes fixed on him, as if they weren't certain what he'd do next, and were determined to keep their eyes on him. "I didn't mean to—"

"I understand it seems ridiculous to you to call our lessons animal husbandry, Lord Hawke. Despite what you may think, I do realize domestic cats don't qualify as livestock. I'm not a fool."

"I don't think you're a—"

"The boys enjoy being in the stables, my lord, and like most young children, they're interested in animals. My intent with these lessons is merely to encourage that interest, and at the same time teach them how to behave towards animals with kindness and compassion."

"I—I wasn't going to take the cat." He'd told her that twice already, and he sounded like a half-wit repeating himself over again, but those were the words that rose to his lips when he turned back to face Miss Templeton. All at once it seemed imperative that someone, at least, understood that much. "I would never take something they loved away from them. Surely, they must know that?"

"How would they know it?" Despite her harsh words, her face had softened a little. "It's been months since they've seen you. That's a lifetime at their age. They aren't certain what you'll do, because they don't know you anymore."

It wasn't a pleasant thing to hear, but hadn't he seen the truth of what she was saying for himself? He might argue with her all he liked, but it wouldn't change a thing. "Tell the boys they can keep their cat, and carry on with their...animal husbandry lessons." It took an effort for him to get *that* out. "I won't interfere again."

He brushed past her and strode toward the stable doors. A blast of frigid air hit him square in the face and crept under the neckline of his coat as he paused there, half-hoping and half-dreading one of the boys would call out to him, asking him not to leave...

Neither of them said a word.

But Miss Templeton did. "Wait, Lord Hawke." He paused without turning around. Footstep approached from behind him, a determined click of a boot heel against the stone floor. "As I said, the boys don't know you anymore, but they *want* to."

He did turn then, startled. It was a kindness in her to tell him that. A kindness he didn't expect, and one he didn't deserve. Not from her.

For the first time, he really *looked* at her. Oh, she had a haughtiness to her, certainly, with that firm little chin and the determined brow, but there was a softness to her mouth, and compassion in those unusual blue gray eyes.

She was rather like Sophie, in some ways. Kind, but with a backbone of pure steel. There weren't, after all, many governesses in England who'd dare to tell their employer his sons were afraid of him. Miss Templeton might be a troublesome, meddling bit of baggage, but she was no coward.

"What happened just now," she waved her hand toward the corner of the stables where Hecate's pen was located. "And yesterday, on the staircase...there are bound to be rough patches as the boys become accustomed to your being here, my lord, but young boys have short memories, and your sons are eager to give you the benefit of the doubt. In the end, these little misunderstandings won't matter much."

He sucked in a breath. She didn't have to tell him any of this. Given the way he'd treated her since he arrived at Hawke's Run, she had every reason in the world to want to keep him far away from her and his boys.

"They talk about you all the time, you know. Why not stay for the lesson? Ryan and Etienne asked you to come, didn't they?"

"Yes." But that was before he'd threatened their cat, and shouted at their beloved governess. No doubt they were eager to see him go now.

"You might learn something you don't know about animal husbandry if you stay," she added, a cautious smile on her lips. "You don't have to touch Hecate."

"I...no, I don't think so." He should have said more —a thank you, at least, for the consideration she'd shown him, but his chest was tight with shame, and all he could think to say was, "You'll tell the boys what I said about Hecate?"

She nodded, but her smile vanished, her brows drawing together in a frown. "I'll tell them, my lord."

He returned to the castle and went straight to his bedchamber, but even the fire leaping in the grate couldn't chase away the chill. He considered ordering another bath, but this chill went deeper than his skin, all the way down to his bones.

Guilt and shame could freeze a man from the in-side out.

The way Ryan and Etienne had looked at him,

when he'd lost his temper with Miss Templeton just now! They'd been truly *frightened* of him, and Ryan had jumped in front of Hecate's pen as if he'd actually believed Adrian might hurt the cat.

God, the shame that had flooded him then...

The past two years had been the bitterest of his life, but he couldn't recall a more bitter moment than that one.

He leapt up and began to pace from one end of his bedchamber to the other. What had Miss Templeton said, about the animal husbandry lessons? That she wanted to teach Ryan and Etienne how to behave with kindness and compassion?

Perhaps his sons weren't the only ones who could benefit from such a lesson. God knew he'd made a bloody mess of things this morning, but he could try again.

Hecate was only a cat. Caring for her was such a tiny, insignificant thing compared to the many ways he'd failed his sons, all he owed them. But at least it was a start, and he had to start somewhere, didn't he?

One limb at a time...

Cats, though. He ran his fingertips over the scratches that little gray creature had carved into his neck, wincing at the sting.

Of all the animals in the world, why did it have to be cats?

CHAPTER
SIX

J ust as Helena had suspected, spending a night with a passel playful kittens locked inside her bedchamber was not as amusing as she'd hoped it would be.

Indeed, after the first hour or two, it ceased to be amusing at all.

She made it into the darkest hours of the early morning before she lost patience entirely, struggled out from underneath the coverlet and made her way across the cold floor to the window seat. "Come along, you wicked things."

A parade of gray, white and black kittens chased after her, their claws catching in the hems of her nightdress. "Here, Hestia. You too, Poseidon." She scooped up the gray kitten in one hand and her brother in the other, and plopped them down into her lap. They were the two worst offenders, forever on the prowl, and riling the others up with their antics. "Now hush."

She and Abby had conducted a diligent search of the castle, poking into every nook and cranny where a naughty kitten might hide, but they'd only managed to find four out of the six of them—Hestia and three of her brothers—but six kittens were more than enough to keep one exhausted governess awake for most of the night.

She tucked herself into the window seat, a pillow behind her back, the view outside the window catching her eye. It was only the stable yard, but the bright winter moon above cast its ethereal rays over the frosty ground, gilding everything with a silvery glow.

She let out a sigh as her gaze wandered to the closed stable door.

Ryan and Etienne had been quiet for a time after Lord Hawke left the stables yesterday morning, but they'd settled soon enough, their attention diverted by Hecate who, for all that she was semi-feral quite enjoyed all the attention she was getting, and had set up a contented purring.

But she hadn't settled down. Lord Hawke's wounded expression had stayed with her long after they'd concluded their animal husbandry lesson and returned to the castle, and it had continued to trouble her throughout the rest of the day, so much so if she'd managed to get even a wink of sleep tonight, he likely would have haunted her dreams.

There was no reason in the world she should take Lord Hawke's troubles so to heart—she didn't even *like* the man—but it seemed a robust aversion to him wasn't enough to chase the memory of his anguished expression from her mind.

It didn't make any sense. She'd never come across a more intolerable man in her life, with his arrogant questions and that superior smirk, and that was to say nothing of his loathing of cats. She didn't trust anyone who didn't like cats. It wasn't *normal*, for pity's sake.

As for that woebegone expression of his, well...did he really deserve her sympathy? Goodness knew he'd brought all his troubles down on his own head. She was a great believer in suffering the consequences of one's own bad behavior, yet for some maddening reason, it didn't seem to matter that Lord Hawke was reaping precisely what he'd sown.

She scratched her nails gently over Poseidon's silky black belly, his drowsy purr vibrating against her fingers.

One thing was certain. She didn't feel the least bit guilty about what had happened with Lord Hawke in the stables. No, of course not. Why should she? It wasn't *her* fault things had taken such an unpleasant turn, even if she had been hoping that very morning that Lord Hawke wouldn't inflict his troublesome presence on them while he remained at Hawke's Run.

But it wasn't as if she'd chased him off when he did appear.

Not at all.

Only...well, she hadn't helped matters much, either, not until the end, and even then, her efforts had been half-hearted. And of course, by the time she exerted herself, it had already been too late. Lord Hawke had slunk out the stable doors like the worst sort of criminal, and she hadn't seen him for the rest of the day.

Not that she'd been looking for him. And it was quite a large castle.

She glanced out into the moonlit stable yard, her fingers still moving absently over the warm bundles of gray and black fur now curled in her lap. The trouble was, she'd made a rather worrying mistake. Despite her lecture about the foolishness of making assumptions, she'd gone ahead and made her own assumptions about him, hadn't she?

She'd assumed it wouldn't matter at all to Lord Hawke if his sons rebuffed him.

He was the one who'd gone off to London to debauch courtesans and wager away his fortune instead of spending time with his motherless sons. Months gone by without a single visit, for pity's sake! Surely, she was justified in thinking he didn't care at all about Ryan and Etienne?

But, justified or not, she'd been wrong. Dead wrong.

Their rebuff *had* mattered to him. Quite a lot, judging by his miserable expression. He'd seemed baffled, too, as if he couldn't quite figure out how it had all gone so dreadfully wrong.

In his way, he'd been trying to connect with the boys. He'd gone about it clumsily enough, but he'd been there, hadn't he? He'd held their hands in his as they'd crossed from the castle to the stable yard, and though he'd been a trifle bemused by their bright chatter, he'd listened eagerly enough, a tolerant half-smile on his lips.

She leaned her head against the window and let out another sigh, her breath leaving a damp film of fog on the glass. The truth was, for all that they were uncertain about him, Ryan and Etienne loved their father, and they needed him. She knew this, yet she'd done little to help mend the rift between them.

Perhaps she could be forgiven for neglecting to read Lord Hawke properly, but there was no excuse for not doing her utmost to reconcile Ryan and Etienne to their father. *She*, of all people, who knew what it was to have a loving, attentive father, how much it meant.

Everything.

She huffed another hazy lungful of air onto the glass, then reached out to trace a finger through it. But how was she meant to fix it? Lord Hawke had made it clear he didn't care for her opinions, and—

She froze as a flicker of movement in the stable yard below caught her eye. "What in the world?" The cats let out sleepy meows of protest as she sprang up onto her knees and peered out the window.

Was that...*yes*! A dark shadow was passing through the stable yard!

But who would be out there at this time of morning? It must be an animal, or...no, there weren't many animals in the Oxfordshire countryside who walked upright. It was certainly a man. A poacher, perhaps? No, that wasn't likely. No thief in his right mind would risk coming this close to the castle.

Whoever it was, he was quite tall, and had exceptionally broad shoulders, and dark hair turned silvery by the moonlight...

"Oh, my goodness!" She slapped a hand over her mouth to smother a gasp.

It was Lord Hawke, sneaking about the stable yard in the dark! Or...no, not the stable yard, but into the stables themselves! Her heart pounded against her ribs as he reached the door, slid it open, and disappeared into the thick darkness inside.

He'd been carrying something, too, hadn't he? There'd been something in his hand. The moonlight had caught a glint of something white. Dear God, he wasn't going after Hecate with ill intent, was he?

No, no. That wasn't it. He'd promised the boys he wouldn't take Hecate away, and for all that she didn't much care for Lord Hawke, she didn't believe he'd lie to Ryan and Etienne. No, he had some other reason, but what? What possible business could he have in the stables at...she glanced at the small clock on the mantel.

Four o'clock in the morning? Why, even Abby wouldn't be up yet!

Whatever he was up to, he didn't want anyone to see him. Oh dear, that *did* seem a bit menacing, didn't it? What did he mean, creeping about his own stable yard like a thief? It didn't make any sense.

She waited, breath held for what felt like forever, but at last the stable door slid open again, and the tall, dark, broad-shouldered shadow reappeared. His back was toward her, and he paused there, as if watching something unfolding inside, then he turned, and a shaft of moonlight caught the lower half of his face, throwing the sharp angles of his jaw and chin and his full lips into sharp relief.

A soft gasp fell from her lips. Yes, there was no mistaking that face. It was Lord Hawke, and he was... well, he rather stole one's breath, didn't he? Strange, that she hadn't noticed how perfect his features were before now, but perhaps he wasn't quite as handsome as that in the daytime?

It must be the moonlight. It flattered everyone.

He stood there in the doorway for some time before he pulled the stable door closed and crept back across the yard back toward the castle, vanishing into the shadows.

Whatever he'd had in his hand was now gone.

Hestia and Poseidon each let out a sleepy howl of

protest as she tumbled them out of the nest they'd made in the lap of her nightdress. "Yes, I do beg your pardon, but something is afoot." She scrambled up from the window seat. "And if you recall, neither of you permitted me a single wink of sleep last night."

She gave each furry head a distracted pat, then hurried into her cloak and boots, and with a quick peek into the hallway outside her bedchamber door, ran down three flights of stairs, through the kitchen and out into the stable yard.

She paused when she reached the stable door, shivering in her nightdress. "Goodness, it's cold." She hadn't bothered with stockings or gloves, so she stamped her feet and blew on her fingers as she darted through the door.

Her heart began to race as she drew closer to the pen at the back of the stables, but Hecate was in her pen, right where they'd left her this morning, rolling about on her back in the hay, as content as ever.

Or, no. *More* content than ever, because there beside her, tucked into the hay was a small, white porcelain dish, with the remains of what looked like...

She dropped to her knees, reached over the side of the pen and snatched it up.

Clotted cream?

No, surely not. She dragged a fingertip through the dregs Hecate had left behind, and touched it to the end of her tongue.

By God, it was!

She sat back on her heels, amazed.

Lord Hawke, the man who claimed to loathe cats with the heat of a thousand suns had left his warm bed, sneaked out into the dark, freezing night, and delivered a bowl of clotted cream to a cat he despised.

"Is Lord Hawke taking his tea now, Mrs. Norris?"

Mrs. Norris had bustled into the kitchen after answering Lord Hawke's summons, and was rummaging about for the tea things. "Hmmm? What's that, Miss Templeton? Oh, the tea. Yes. Will you set the kettle on, Abby, and bring his lordship his tea?"

"Yes, Mrs. Norris." Abby lifted the kettle onto the stove, then hurried back to puzzling over the note Cook had left with the instructions for the pastry tomorrow morning. It was her half day, so the morning baking was left to Abby.

"I can't make any sense of this!" Abby wailed, waving the note in the air. "What does this say?"

Helena leaned over her shoulder and peered at the note. Really, Cook had the most deplorable handwriting. It was no wonder poor Abby was always in fits over it. "I believe that says currants."

"Does it, indeed?" Abby squinted at the paper. "Yes, I think you're right. Currant scones. I'd better get this dough prepared, or I'll be behind tomorrow morning."

Helena lingered beside the kitchen table, waiting until Mrs. Norris bustled back out again, then said to Abby, "Would it help if I brought Lord Hawke his tea?"

"Would you? That would help ever so much, and save me from one of his scowls, too!" Abby turned a beaming smile on her, but then her brow clouded. "Are you quite sure, Miss Templeton? He scowls at you even more fiercely than he does me."

He did, indeed, but she'd gladly face his scowls for

a chance to prod him about the curious incident she'd witnessed this morning. Well, she couldn't prod him, exactly—a governess didn't prod an earl—but she'd think of something.

She'd waited all day for a chance to speak to him, but it was almost as if he knew what she was up to, because the contrary man had contrived to stay well out of sight today. He'd risen early, made his way down the stairs to his study, and hadn't emerged again for the rest of the day.

Now, at last, Mrs. Norris was busy with the up-stairs housemaids, the boys were engaged with their music master, and Abby was distracted with her cur-rant scones. She wouldn't get another chance like this. "Certainly, I'm sure. Lord Hawke's scowls don't trouble me, Abby. Is there any lemon cake?"

Perhaps a thick slice of lemon cake would sweeten his temper.

"He doesn't care for lemon cake with his tea. Mrs. Norris says he's not fond of sweets, but prefers a plain seed cake. Can you imagine?" Abby shook her head as she busily loaded a plate with a few slices of beef and salmon, and some cheese with bread and butter. "His townhouse is in Berkeley Square, too, not far from Gunther's! Rather a waste, really."

"Indeed, it's unforgivable of him." Helena snatched up the tray as soon as Abby had settled the plate on it, and hurried toward the kitchen door.

"Wait, Miss Templeton!"

Helena turned, trying to hide her impatience. "Yes, what it is, Abby?"

"You forgot the tea." Abby held up the teapot.

"Oh, dear, so I did! Goodness, what a goose I am.

Here, put it on the end there, won't you? Right, I'll just deliver this, then, shall I?"

Abby was already back to her scones, and waved her off. "Yes, but mind the stairs with that tray!"

"For pity's sake, it was one time." Still, she did take care on the kitchen stairs, as she didn't fancy another trayful of broken porcelain, and made her way down the corridor to Lord Hawke's study.

"Come," he called gruffly in response to her knock.

"Your tea, Lord Hawke."

He blinked up at her, pausing in whatever he'd been writing. "You're the governess, Miss Templeton, not a housemaid. Why are you delivering my tea?"

"Mrs. Norris and Abby were taken up with other duties, and I was coming this way to fetch the boys from the music room in any case, so I offered to bring it with me. Where shall I put it?"

"Just there, on the edge of the desk."

She did as he asked, and he went back to his work, but when she didn't leave after depositing the tea tray, he looked up again with a frown. "Is there something else you needed, Miss Templeton?"

She stared at him, a curious dryness in her throat. It hadn't just been the flattering effects of the moonlight on his face that had stolen her breath this morning. Even in the dim light of his study, there was no denying Lord Hawke was an extraordinarily handsome man.

Goodness, she must have been making a rather strenuous effort not to have noticed it before, but it was as if that glimpse of his face outside the stables this morning had caught her off guard, and now she *had* noticed it, she couldn't...well, un-notice it.

Of course, *she* wasn't one to be swayed by a handsome face. His piercing green eyes and firm jaw didn't make Lord Hawke any less of an arrogant, intolerable aristocrat.

An arrogant, intolerable aristocrat who braved the freezing cold to bring a dish of clotted cream to a pregnant cat—

"Miss Templeton?" He set his pen down carefully on his desk. "I asked if there's something else you needed."

"Needed? Er, no. No, indeed, I just...well, I thought you might like to accompany Ryan and Etienne to the stables tomorrow morning."

"More animal husbandry?"

Oh, dear. He didn't sound at all enthusiastic. "Yes. We'll go every day now, as Hecate is approximately fifty-eight days along, and is thus nearing the window at which she's most likely to give birth, so—"

"Forgive me, Miss Templeton, but I could quite happily live the rest of my life without ever knowing the details of the feline birth cycle."

"But—"

He held up a hand. "I distinctly recall you warning me not to interfere with your lessons, and I've told you more than once, Miss Templeton, that I despise cats."

Who was he attempting to convince of that, her, or himself? "But Ryan and Etienne want you there, my lord."

"Why, because it went so well the first time?"

He shook his head, but underneath the sarcastic smile on his lips was a hint of that same misery she'd noticed the other day, and her chest tightened. Much like his handsome face, now she'd seen it, she couldn't *unsee* it, and it didn't sit well with her.

Not at all.

"If they didn't want you there, Lord Hawke, they never would have asked you to come the first time. I admit it was a bit awkward, but if you'll only give it another chance, I'm certain it will—"

"No, thank you, Miss Templeton. I think it's best for all of us if I stay well away from the stables."

"It *isn't* what's best for everyone!" And if he truly wanted to stay away, then why was he sneaking about the stables at night? "Please, Lord Hawke, if you'd just give it another—"

"You're dismissed, Miss Templeton." He picked up his pen, and bent over the papers scattered across his desk. "Please close the door on your way out."

CHAPTER
SEVEN

Hecate wasn't, as cats went, the worst creature Adrian had ever encountered.

She was still a cat, of course, and thus was moody and unpredictable like most of her species, but Ryan and Etienne were right. She didn't scratch or bite, and she did have remarkably soft, warm fur.

Not that he'd patted her. She'd brushed up against his hand, that's all.

She seemed to tolerate his visits well enough, though that had more to do with the clotted cream and bits of meat than any desire she had for his charming company. Still, the welcoming meow she gave him when he entered the stables now wasn't entirely disagreeable.

"Hungry, are you?" He stepped into the pen, spread an old horse blanket over the hay and settled down beside her. "I do hope tonight's offering agrees with you, madam."

Hecate had a rather discriminating palate, for a cat. He'd made the mistake of bringing her French beans a la crème the other night. She'd given them a disinterested sniff, then turned her back on him, disgusted by his stupidity.

He hadn't made *that* mistake again.

"It's a nice ragout this evening. I liberated it from my dinner plate, but don't tell Cook that." He rummaged in his coat pocket, took out the napkin he'd hidden there and spread the morsels out on the floor. "Here we are."

Hecate rose from her sprawl, sniffed delicately at the beef, and after a fastidious twitch of her nose, deemed it acceptable. He reclined back against the side of the pen and watched, oddly pleased, as she began to eat. "That's it. There's a good cat."

Good cat, indeed. If his fashionable London friends could see him now, they'd either laugh themselves sick, or drag him directly off to Bedlam. God knew he didn't bear much resemblance to the elegant Earl of Hawke *now*, with his breeches dusted with hay and bits of Hecate's orange fur stuck to his coat.

Even now, three nights into his feline experiment, he hadn't any bloody idea what he was doing here, hunkered down in the hay, his arse gone numb with cold in spite of the horse blanket, trying to make friends with a persnickety cat.

A *cat*, of all absurd things.

But Hecate wasn't just any cat. She was *Ryan* and *Etienne's* cat.

After eight long months of absence from Hawke's Run, he no longer knew how to talk to his sons. He didn't know how to be with them—he didn't know them at all anymore, really—and since he'd returned home, his efforts to bridge the gap seemed destined for disaster. He couldn't bear to see their eager expectation give way to bitter disappointment every time they gave him another chance, and he made another gaffe.

The fear was even worse. He'd seen it on their faces—that flash of uncertainty, that nearly imperceptible flinch backwards.

Cats were sly, demanding creatures, but they were a great deal less complicated than little boys were. If he could persuade Hecate to tolerate him without utterly cocking the thing up, then there might be hope for him, after all.

It was a start, at least. Proof that the thing could be done.

He rested his head against the side of Hecate's pen and stared up at the dusty rafters above. Aside from Hecate's soft nibbling and the whistle of the wind around the sides of the stables, it was silent here.

It was unnerving, all the silence. There was forever someone nattering in his ear in London, and an endless parade of willing ladies and bored gentlemen traipsing through his townhouse, all of them eager to be seen with the fashionable Lord Hawke.

It was no wonder his sons found him such a disappointment. It had been months since he'd been obliged to exert any effort to please anyone aside from himself. The irony there, of course, was that nothing and no one could please him—

"Mrreowww."

He glanced up at Hecate's disgruntled meow. "Yes? What is it *now*? No, I don't have any more beef, you greedy creature."

She ambled over to him, her heavy belly hanging low, and without so much as a by- your-leave crawled into his lap and settled herself down on top of him as if he were a stuffed cushion.

"No, that won't do. Bad cat." It was ridiculous enough he was sneaking into the stables at night to feed her, but a cat lounging atop him, kneading her claws on his thigh? No, indeed. He did have *some* pride left. "This isn't part of our agreement, Hecate."

Hecate paused to glare at him with her round, yellow eyes, then began calmly licking her paw.

"You're spoiling my coat, you ridiculous animal." It was a Weston, for God's sake. He wriggled his legs, trying to dislodge her, and when that didn't work, he rolled onto his side to tip her off. "Go on, shoo."

But Hecate didn't shoo. She remained right where she was, a continuous rumble emanating from her throat.

Well, it *was* quite cold tonight, and then Hecate was fifty-four days into her gestational cycle—at least, according to Miss Templeton's charts. Perhaps it wouldn't hurt for him to let her lounge on top of him for a bit.

He settled back against the pen and curled his hand around Hecate's back. Miss Templeton and her infernal charts. Yesterday, she'd brought Hecate's gestational chart with her when she brought him his tea, just in case he wished to 'have a look at it.'

He didn't, of course. The very idea was absurd. If he *had* taken a peek at it once she was gone, it was only because she'd left it on his desk, where he couldn't avoid seeing it.

No doubt precisely as she intended it.

He'd never met a more persistent woman than Miss Templeton in his life. He couldn't make the least sense of her. She should have been pleased to be rid of him after the way he'd behaved toward her, but instead she seemed utterly determined to lure him back to the stables for another animal husbandry lesson.

Animal husbandry, indeed. More like cat coddling.

Still, he hadn't liked the way her face had fallen when he'd dismissed her, and after she'd gone, he'd had rather a lot of trouble settling down to his work again. Then this morning he'd found himself watching her, Ryan and Etienne march down the pathway from the castle to the stables with a twinge in his chest...

God above. First the cat, and now the meddlesome governess. Either being at Hawke's Run was having a decidedly bad effect on him, or a decidedly good one. He hadn't yet made up his mind.

One thing was certain, however. Hecate's purring was lulling him to sleep. "I do beg your pardon for disturbing you, Hecate, but as much as I treasure our newfound friendship, I draw the line at spending the night in the stables."

He didn't draw the line at leaving her his coat, however, and she'd burrowed quite contentedly into its folds by the time he left the stables, closing the door against the biting wind on his way out. He'd have to fetch it early tomorrow morning. It wouldn't do for Miss Templeton and the boys to find it there—

"Mew, mew, mew."

What the devil? He paused halfway across the stable yard, listening, but the mewling was gone. All he heard was the wailing of the wind.

Damn it, he was hearing cats everywhere now.

He resumed his trek across the yard, his boots crunching over the thick layer of frost on the ground, but when he neared the kitchen door he heard it again—a frightened, pathetic mewling, and it was growing more desperate every moment.

It was certainly a cat, but it couldn't be Hecate. She was tucked safely into her pen inside the stables, and it was too high-pitched, more like a kitten's cry. But where the devil *was* it?

"Mew, mew, mew."

Bloody hell. The kitten was nearby, but it was as dark as Hades out here, and by the sounds of it, it was a tiny thing, and likely hiding from him. "Here, kitty. Come on out, now."

There was another pitiful mewl, then a tiny shape detached itself from the shadows near the kitchen door and took a hesitant step toward him.

Oh, no. It was that little gray demon, the one who'd sliced the back of his neck to ribbons! Miss Templeton's cat. Hera, was it? No, that wasn't right, but it was something like that. Whatever her name was, there was no question Miss Templeton loved the little vagrant. She'd nearly sacrificed her position for the cat after that incident on the staircase with the drinking chocolate.

Damn it, why did it have to be this particular cat? She'd likely make mincemeat of his fingers if he tried to touch her, yet he couldn't very well leave her out here. She'd freeze to death, and that was assuming an owl or coyote didn't get her first.

Even he wasn't so hard-hearted as to leave her to such a sad fate. With one last prayer for the well-being of his fingers, he crouched down and held out his hand to her. "Come here, little creature. Yes, that's it. Nice kitty—"

For all that the kitten was a demon from the underworld, she was no fool. She saw at once he was her best and only hope of rescue, and scurried toward him. He scooped her up in one hand—she was no bigger than his palm—and held her against his chest to protect her from the wind. As quick as lightning she scrambled up his shirt front, settled herself under his chin, and nestled her tiny body into the hollow of his throat.

"Er, well, alright, then. I suppose that will do." She hadn't scratched him, and she was already purring, and the sensation of her warm, soft body tucked against him wasn't *awful*.

But now that he had her, what was he meant to *do* with her? Leave her in the kitchen? Or outside Miss Templeton's bedchamber, so she'd be sure to see her when she woke? He made his way through the dark kitchen, the kitten still cuddled under his chin, but paused when he reached the bottom of the entryway staircase.

He couldn't go wandering about in the hallway outside Miss Templeton's bedchamber. It wasn't proper. That is, he didn't have any wicked intent towards his governess, of course. It was all perfectly innocent—of course, it was—but what if she heard him out there, and came into the corridor clad only in her night rail?

Miss Templeton in a night rail...no, nothing good would come of *that*.

He curled his hand around the kitten's body, intending to detach her from his person and leave her at the bottom of the stairs, where she'd surely be safe until someone found her in the morning, but the kitten had no desire to leave the warm place she'd found. She clung to the collar of his shirt with her tiny claws and let out a mewl so pathetic it pierced even his stony heart.

Now what? He wasn't taking her to his own bedchamber. It was out of the question. "Be reasonable, er..." Was her name Hebe? Or Hermana? It was some Greek goddess's name, but damned if he could remember what. "You don't want to come up with me. We're sworn enemies, remember?"

But the kitten *didn't* remember, because she only snuggled closer, one paw resting against the curve of his neck. "For God's sake. Very well, then, but only for one night—"

"Hestia?" There was a soft shuffle of footsteps on the stairs above, then, "Dash it, you naughty girl, where have you gotten to?"

He looked up, and there, at the top of the second-floor landing was Miss Templeton, dressed in a white night rail, her long, thick hair hanging loose around her shoulders.

He gazed up at her, his mouth going dry.

She wasn't wearing *just* her night rail—a circumstance that was both extremely lucky and extremely disappointing at once—but had a pair of half-boots on her feet and a cloak over her shoulders. Yet the sight of Miss Templeton in her night rail, with her hair floating in a golden-brown cloud around her wasn't a sight he'd soon forget, boots and cloak be damned.

The truth hit him all at once then, like a sudden blow to the stomach, snatching the breath from his lungs. His instant and inexplicable dislike of her. His ill-temper toward her, his teasing and goading and generally dreadful behavior...

He wanted her. He *wanted* Helena Templeton.

He wanted her from the first moment he'd caught sight of her in that tree, in her worn boots and that catastrophe of a yellow cloak. Why had he handled it so badly? He was a man, for God's sake, not a boy. In some circles he was even considered charming, but he hadn't been charming to *her*.

No, to *her*, he'd behaved like an utter arse. Why, it was as bad as if he'd been tugging on her curls and splashing mud on her pinafores like an infatuated prepubescent boy who'd fallen victim to a pretty face.

Why hadn't he known it at once as desire? It wasn't as if she were the first woman he'd ever wanted. The answer slammed into him like another blow to the stomach.

Because he hadn't desired anyone since Sophie.

No, it was more than that. He hadn't believed he ever *could* desire another woman after Sophie, and now here was Miss Templeton—his sons' governess, of all absurd things—her wild curls and those fascinating blue gray eyes holding him captive—

"Lord Hawke? Oh, dear, I...er, I beg your pardon." She pulled her cloak tighter around her shoulders, a flush rising in her cheeks. "I didn't expect anyone else would be awake. Hestia escaped from my rooms, you see, and I—"

Hestia, of course! The little creature's name was Hestia. "Yes, I have her. I found her outside the kitchen door, crying."

"Oh, thank you, my lord! I was dreadfully worried about her. She doesn't usually leave my bedchamber."

"Well, I don't think she'll venture to do so again. She was rather terrified when I found her, and now she, ah...she won't let go of my shirt."

"Here, let me help. She'll come to me I think." She hurried down the stairs, stopping three steps from the bottom so they were eye to eye. "Come here, Hestia. It's alright."

He stilled as she reached for the kitten, her crooning voice winding around his chest before dipping low and settling in the pit of his stomach. He swallowed. "She's still clinging to my shirt. You, ah... you may have to help get her off."

"Yes, of course." Her blue-gray eyes met his for an instant, and she caught her lower lip between her teeth, the flush on her cheeks deepening. "Come here, sweetheart."

She slid her fingers under Hestia's tiny belly, her fingers brushing against his neck, and he smothered a groan. She was his sons' governess, for God's sake. His sons' governess. He repeated the warning in his head as she gently disentangled the kitten from his shirt, and dear God, it felt like she was touching him everywhere, her fingertips stroking the sensitive place behind his ear, her fingernails scratching lightly against his neck as she urged the kitten away from him.

By the time she gathered Hestia against her chest, his own fingers were twitching to wrap around her waist, and beads of sweat were sliding down the back of his neck. "There, Hestia," he said. "You're all right now."

"It was kind of you to bring her inside, Lord Hawke." She glanced shyly up at him from under her lashes. "I, ah...I know she's not your favorite animal."

He shrugged, but his head was still swimming from her touch. "Come now, Miss Templeton. I never said she was all *that* terrible."

She blinked up at him, then the corner of those delectable lips quirked into a grin. "You called her a demonic hellcat."

He'd called her worse, too, but fortunately not in Miss Templeton's hearing. "Yes, well, she's rather grown on me since then."

She studied him for a moment, her fingers slowly stroking over Hestia's sleek gray back. "They do tend to do that, don't they, Lord Hawke?"

Something in her gaze made heat rise in his cheeks. "Yes, well, I wouldn't get my hopes up if I were you, Miss Templeton. I still don't like cats."

"Don't you? Well, that's an improvement over detesting them, at least." Her grin widened. "I daresay by this time next week you'll be as devoted of a slave to them as the rest of us at Hawke's Run."

He snorted. "I wouldn't count on it." Though it wasn't quite as ludicrous a notion as it had been three days ago.

"Hmmm." With that enigmatic reply, she gathered Hestia tighter against her chest, and turned to make her way up the stairs. He was struggling against the urge not to watch her go and failing miserably when she reached the landing, paused and turned to face him. "A question, if I might, Lord Hawke?"

"Yes, what is it?"

"What were you doing outdoors?"

"I, er..." Damn it, his mind was utterly blank. "What do you mean, Miss Templeton? I wasn't outdoors."

"But you said you found Hestia outside the kitchen door, my lord." She arched an eyebrow. "And you have your boots on."

Damn the woman. Did nothing escape her notice?

Just as he was certain he was going to have to confess his furtive stable excursions, however, inspiration struck. "I might ask you the same question, Miss Templeton. Why are you wearing your cloak and boots?"

"I...I thought Hestia might have gone outside."

"Indeed? It seems strange you would think so, given how far your bedchamber is from an outside door."

She didn't say anything for a moment, but just when he thought she'd march off back to her bedchamber, those full, plump lips he'd no doubt dream about tonight quirked with another grin. "Perhaps, but it wouldn't be the only strange occurrence this evening, would it, Lord Hawke?"

"No, indeed. Not the only strange occurrence." Not by any measure.

She hesitated, then asked, "You, ah, you didn't happen to see a black kitten down there anywhere, did you, my lord?"

"A black kitten? What, you mean to say there's a black one, too?" How many kittens was she hiding in his castle?

"Er, never mind, my lord. Goodnight!" With that, she turned and fled up the last few steps, Hestia peering down at him over her shoulder.

"Goodnight, Miss Templeton," he murmured as she disappeared around the corner. "Sweet dreams."

CHAPTER
EIGHT

The day after Helena's strange encounter with Lord Hawke passed uneventfully, one hour following after the next in a busy blur of lessons with the boys until the frosty afternoon gave way to a quiet, peaceful evening.

But the wee hours of the following morning, those dark, still hours before the sun ventured over the horizon, well...they were another matter entirely.

Helena waited until the mantel clock chimed four times before she tossed back the coverlet and rose from her bed. It was dreadfully early, and Hestia and Poseidon had once again kept her awake for hours the night before with their antics, but she wasn't plagued with grogginess and bleary eyes this morning.

No, this time, she was wide awake.

She crept across the room, dropped into the window seat and folded her legs underneath her, knowing what she'd see before she glanced into the grounds below.

That is, *whom* she'd see, despite the early hour.

Lord Hawke didn't seem to have the least idea how to behave like a proper dissipated earl. Perhaps when he was in London he spent every hour of his day like every other nobleman—that is, with sleeping, dressing and debauchery, but since he'd arrived at Hawke's Run, he'd been astonishingly productive of a morning.

He didn't appear at once, but the clock hadn't yet chimed the quarter hour before he was striding across the stable yard dressed only in his shirtsleeves and breeches, with a coat thrown over his shoulders, his dark hair mussed and bits of hay stuck to his boots.

She pressed closer to the window, so close the tip of her nose touched the cold glass, and braced her hand on the window sill, her breath held as the tall, broad shape approached the stable doors. He had something in his arms today. She couldn't make out what it was from here, but it looked heavy—far too heavy to be merely a handful of treats—but it was certainly another offering to Hecate.

A velvet cushion, perhaps, or silk hanging for the sides of her pen? She pressed a hand to her mouth to smother a snort, but really, it wasn't as far-fetched as it seemed.

It had been the cream, the first time. She'd caught him out at that easily enough because he'd left the dish behind, but he'd grown cagier since that first morning, and she'd been obliged to paw about in the hay to find the remains of the morning's treats.

Yesterday, it had been bits of salmon cutlet, though she might never have figured it out if Hecate, who was nothing if not discriminating hadn't left the capers behind. The day before she'd found traces of what looked suspiciously like the pigeon pie they'd eaten for dinner the previous night. She'd even found a shriveled French bean, buried under the hay in a corner of the pen.

Cook would have a fit if she ever found out about *that*. She was a bit sensitive about her French beans.

But it wasn't just the treats. Each time she ventured into the stables after he'd gone, she found fresh hay spread over the floor of Hecate's pen, with Hecate enthroned upon it, purring loudly like a satisfied princess. For a gentleman who claimed to despise cats, Lord Hawke was awfully solicitous of Hecate's comfort.

Strange doings, indeed.

She waited until Lord Hawke vanished into the stables, then flopped back down on the window seat. The maddening part was, as soon as daylight dawned, he was as aloof as he'd ever been, every inch the arrogant earl. If she hadn't seen him herself, she never would have believed the demanding Earl of Hawke was the same man who was feeding bits of his dinner to a pregnant cat.

It was as if he were two different people.

It didn't matter how much she poked and prodded, Lord Hawke wouldn't confess a single word about his early morning visits to the stables. She'd brought him his tea for three afternoons in a row now, just so she might have a private moment to tease him into revealing himself, but no amount of hinting and wheedling would open the man's stubborn lips.

She'd all but begged him to join her and the boys for another animal husbandry lesson, and even brought Hecate's chart to his study in hopes of catching him out. In short, she'd given him every opportunity she could think of to admit he wasn't the hard-hearted, cat-loathing man he pretended to be, all to no avail.

Why would he want to hide such a thing? It didn't make *sense*, dash it.

Things that didn't make sense irked her, and especially so in *his* case. No sooner did she make up her mind he was the most wretched man alive than she'd catch a glimpse of humanity under that snarling exterior.

Well, she'd had enough of it.

This morning would mark the final day of Lord Hawke's sneaking about. Today, she was going to confront him with the evidence of his own kindness. Let him try and deny it when she presented him with a handful of soggy bits of last night's pork a la Boisseau.

The mantel clock had just chimed the five o'clock hour when Lord Hawke emerged from the stables, made his way back across the yard and disappeared into the castle. It would be ages yet before the boys rose from their beds. That left her plenty of time to sneak into the stables, paw about in the hay until she found what he'd brought Hecate, and then present him with the proof.

She abandoned her place in the window seat, hurried into her clothes and tiptoed down the dark staircase, pausing when she reached the bottom, but there was no sign of Lord Hawke, and his study door was closed. So, she hurried downstairs to the kitchen, let herself out the back door, and ran down the pathway to the stables.

Goodness, it was cold! She clapped her hands together to warm them, frosty clouds drifting from her lips and her boots slipping over the icy ground as she made her way to the stable door and slipped inside, pausing for a moment to listen.

Yes, there it was, the low, rhythmic buzz that had become so familiar of late.

It was Hecate, and she was purring. Loudly.

"What's he brought you this time, you smug little thing?" She knelt in front of the pen, and stoked a careful hand over the silky orange fur. "You're certainly pleased about something."

Whatever Lord Hawke had left this time was well-hidden, however, and Hecate wasn't telling his secrets. She scrambled about, pushing the hay this way and that, but either Lord Hawke had failed Hecate this morning, or the dratted cat had already devoured all the evidence.

What now, then? Dash it, there was nothing else for it but to wait until tomorrow, and try again. How excessively tiresome! But she couldn't find what wasn't there—

Wait, what was that? A corner of something dark was sticking out from under Hecate's right paw. Keeping an eye on the cat, she slid her hand underneath the furry body, and her fingertips landed on a thick, soft flannel.

There was something else, as well, something hard and warm, like...

No, it couldn't be! How would he ever even think of it?

But it was. She lifted up the edge of the flannel, and there they were, arranged in a circle, the thick flannel over them to protect Hecate from their rough surface.

Bricks. He'd laid warmed bricks down on the stable floor, then covered them with the flannel blanket. And there was Hecate, lounging in the middle of this heated nest for all the world as if she were luxuriating in a warm bath!

She fell back onto her heels, shaking her head. Warmed bricks, of all things. She'd gone to great pains to see to it that Hecate was comfortable during her lying-in, but it had never even occurred to her to supply the cat with warmed bricks.

How in the world, then, had it *ever* occurred to Lord Hawke? And once it had, what had possessed him to see it through? It was no small effort to warm half a dozen bricks and then drag them from the castle all the way to the stables.

But here was the proof that he'd done just that, right here in front of her.

Not more than a week ago, she would have sworn he wasn't at all the sort to trouble himself much about another's creature's comfort, whether human or feline. She would have described him as a cross, curmudgeonly sort of man, a spoiled London rake, and a father of two lovely boys he didn't seem to care a whit about.

But with every day that passed, she saw how wrong she was, and how arrogant to imagine she could know him from a single week's acquaintance. What did she really know about Lord Hawke, when it came down to it?

Not much, even now, but one thing was certain. A man who truly *didn't* care about his sons wouldn't dream of going to such lengths to spoil the pet they adored.

"Enjoy your bath, Hecate." She gave the sleek ginger fur another stroke, snatched up one of the warm bricks

—quite a tangible piece of evidence, that—then gathered up her skirts, struggled to her feet and slipped from the stables back across the stable yard, up the kitchen staircase and down the corridor to Lord Hawke's study.

The door was still closed. She pressed her ear to it, but there was nothing but silence from the other side. She raised her hand, but paused before her knuckles struck the wood.

Was it wise to question Lord Hawke? Or was she making a mistake, interfering in his private business? Really, it was nothing to do with her if he wanted to stuff Hecate full of salmon cutlets.

But of course, this wasn't truly about Hecate.

No, it was about the boys. Surely, they *were* her business?

For all his sneaking about and spoiling Hecate, nothing had changed between Ryan and Etienne and their father. Lord Hawke had kept well away from his sons this past week. She hadn't devoted much study to the impulses of the human mind, but it didn't take an expert in psychology to see Hecate was merely a proxy for Ryan and Etienne—that Lord Hawke was lavishing all the care and affection he didn't dare lavish on his sons on the cat.

The trouble was, it wasn't her place to analyze Lord Hawke. He was the earl, for pity's sake. He might do as he pleased without a word of explanation to anyone, least of all his sons' governess.

Yet even as that thought drifted through her mind her hand lifted, and this time her knuckles met the wood in a sharp rap.

Alas, she'd never been much good at minding her own affairs.

There was a brief pause, then Lord Hawke's surly voice. "What is it?"

Oh, dear. He sounded as if he was in a foul humor, and she hadn't even entered the study yet. She braced herself, and opened the door. "Lord Hawke? Might I have a word with you?"

There was a low fire burning in the grate, but he hadn't lit a lamp. His face was cast in shadows, but there was no mistaking the exasperation in his tone. "It's still dark out, Miss Templeton. What could possibly have happened this early in the morning that requires my attention?"

Perhaps she should have waited until after he'd had his coffee? But she was no coward, and she'd come this far. She wouldn't back out now. "I wish to have a word with you about Hecate, my lord."

"Hecate? You mean that wild cat who's sitting in as livestock for your animal husbandry lessons? Whatever the problem is, I don't know why you're troubling *me* with it. I don't have anything to do with Hecate."

My, he *was* a convincing liar, wasn't he? "That's not quite true, is it, Lord Hawke?"

"I have no idea what you mean, Miss Templeton."

"I think you do." She stepped further into the room and closed the door quietly behind her. "Cream, Lord Hawke. Salmon cutlets, and pigeon pie." She counted the items off on her fingers, one by one. "French beans—I own I don't quite understand that one—and this morning..." She held up the brick she'd taken from Hecate. "Warmed bricks and a soft flannel."

He stared at her for a moment without speaking, but just when she was certain he was about to toss her out of his study, he rose from behind his desk and stalked across the room until he was looming over her. "Have you been spying on me, Miss Templeton?"

Dear God, but he was tall, wasn't he? Had he always been this tall? And his eyes...they were such a piercing green it felt as if he could see down to the depths of her soul. A shiver darted down her spine, but she lifted her chin and met his gaze. "No, I...I came across it quite by accident, I assure you. My bedchamber window looks onto the stable yard, my lord. I've seen you going into the stables myself."

"And followed after me, from the sounds of it. My, you are a sneaky one, aren't you?" He took another step closer, close enough so the damp sleeve of his coat brushed her arm, and the scent of frost and clean hay surrounded her. "In fact, you *have* been spying on me."

"N-not with any ill-intent. I thought..." Oh, *what* had she thought? She hardly knew anymore. Every rational argument had scattered in the wake of his nearness. She couldn't think at all, couldn't breathe, and she turned her head away, desperate to escape those searching green eyes.

"Yes?" He caught her chin between his fingers and turned her face back to his. "What did you think?"

His fingertips were warm and slightly rough against her skin, and the way he was looking at her, the timbre of his voice, husky and deeper than usual...

She'd heard him use that rough voice before, yesterday morning when he'd brought Hestia back to her. The same current she'd felt leaping between them then was there again, writhing between them like a live thing, and he was gazing at her lips, his pupils darkening, his eyelids lowering...

Dear God, was he going to kiss her?

"Oh." Her own eyelids fluttered closed as his thumb came up and traced her lower lip. It was the lightest, gentlest stroke, hardly a touch at all, but somehow it echoed across every inch of her body, making her blood hum in response and a steady pulse beat deep inside her belly.

But he was a rake, wasn't he? How could she have forgotten that? He knew how to touch a woman, how to seduce her, and—

"I asked you a question, Helena. What did you think when you saw me sneaking into the stables in the mornings? Were you afraid for poor Hecate's safety? Did you think I meant to do away with her?"

"I—I didn't know what to think, at first, but now...oh." She caught her breath as he traced her lip again, thrown entirely off her guard at the exquisite sensations flooding through her in response. How could a man reduce her to a quivering mass of need with a single stroke of his thumb?

"Yes? You didn't know what to think, but now...?"

"I—the cream, and the blankets, and the salmon...I think you want to care for someone, and it's easier to care for Hecate than Ryan and Etienne." She forced herself to open her heavy eyelids and meet his gaze. "I think you're either afraid to show how much you care for your sons, or else you don't know how to, so you lavish all your tenderness for them on Hecate, instead."

He stilled, his thumb ceasing its slow stroke across her lips.

"But you don't need to do that, my lord." She searched his inscrutable face, tried to see beyond the shadows that distorted the truth, to see to the man

94

underneath, the one he hid from everyone. "The boys *want* your attention. They miss their father."

He let out a hoarse laugh. "You're a governess, Miss Templeton. You should know that what a child wants isn't always the best thing for them."

"But not this time, my lord," she whispered. "They need you as much as you need them."

He gazed down at her, his throat working, but whatever he wanted to say never made it past his lips. Instead, his hand dropped away from her face. "You needn't worry about Hecate, Miss Templeton." He retreated behind his desk again, his back to her as he stared out the window into the dark, frozen garden. "I can assure you I don't intend her any harm."

Did he truly think she believed he'd hurt Hecate? "I know that, my lord. Will you...will you at least come to the animal husbandry lesson today? The boys want you there."

"I'll think about it. For now, you're dismissed, Miss Templeton."

He'd dismissed her from his presence every time she'd ventured into his study, but this time, it was different. Instead of his usual abruptness, this time he sounded...sad, and her heart gave a wrench in her chest.

Why had this come to matter so much to her? When did it become as much about Lord Hawke as it was about Ryan and Etienne? "Yes, my lord."

She paused, but he didn't turn around when she opened the door. Once she was on the other side she leaned back against it, touching her fingertips to her lips. She didn't have any more answers than she had when she'd entered the study.

Only more questions.

CHAPTER
NINE

Adrian didn't join Miss Templeton for Ryan and Etienne's feline husbandry lesson that afternoon, but kept to himself for the remainder of the day. The worst of it was, he was no longer sure whether it was his sons he was avoiding, or Helena Templeton.

Either way, he soon had cause to regret it, because by the time he did venture from his study, cursing himself as a coward, Miss Templeton had disappeared.

She didn't appear with his tea tray that afternoon, and any hopes he might have secretly entertained that she'd come to the stables early the following morning were dashed when he entered, and found only Cyrus and Hecate. He would have sworn he felt the weight of Helena's gaze on him as he crossed the stable yard, but her bedchamber window was dark, and she didn't appear.

By mid-morning, the walls of his study were closing in on him, and he was so consumed with thoughts of, er...feline husbandry nothing in the world could have stopped him from hurrying to the stables for the lesson.

But when he got there, Miss Templeton was nowhere to be found, and neither were his sons. Hecate cheered up when he appeared, but once she found he didn't have any more of the prawns he'd fed her earlier that morning, she gave a dismissive twitch of her tail that was downright offensive, and proceeded to ignore him.

Where the devil could Miss Templeton have gone? He never should have touched her yesterday. What had he been thinking, stroking her lips in that shameless manner? He'd likely frightened her to death. After such a lapse in propriety, he'd hardly blame her if she left her post!

At the very least, he could have attended the feline husbandry lesson. She'd invited him a half-dozen times this week. Yesterday she'd come close to pleading with him, her lovely blue-gray eyes wide with hope, only for him to disappoint her once again.

He trudged back to the castle and roamed aimlessly from room to room. Eventually he found the boys engaged in a rather chaotic fencing lesson with their beleaguered fencing master, but there was no sign of Miss Templeton. She wasn't in the kitchens, the schoolroom, or the library. He even went so far as to knock on her bedchamber door, but there was no reply.

By the time he came across Mrs. Norris in the linen room, he was all but certain Miss Templeton had left his employ and fled Hawke's Run in the dead of night, so she never had to see his face again. "Mrs. Norris! Miss Templeton is missing!"

Mrs. Norris paused in her inspection of the linen closet. "Missing, my lord?"

"Yes, damn it. I've been all over the house searching for her, from the kitchens to the library to the boys' bedchamber, and even the attics. She's nowhere to be found."

Mrs. Norris stared at him. "The, ah...the attics?"

"Yes! Unless she's hiding in one of the priest's holes underneath the castle, then she's vanished, I tell you!"

"I assure you that Miss Templeton hasn't vanished, my lord. Today is her day off."

"Her day off?" That did make more sense than the priest's hole, didn't it? "I, ah...I see. But don't you mean her half-day?" Surely, she wasn't going to be gone for the entire day?

"No, my lord. Miss Templeton and I arranged for her to take a full day every other week, rather than a half day every week, so she might have time to go and visit her sister at Steeple Cross."

"Steeple Cross? What, has Lord Cross opened the house again?" And why would Miss Templeton's sister be there? Was she the housekeeper there, or the new countess's lady's maid?

"Yes, my lord. He spends a great deal more time there since he married."

Ah. Now he thought of it, he did recall hearing something about Cross having married, to some lady named...well, he couldn't recall what her name was. He hadn't paid much attention, as he and Cross weren't well acquainted, despite being neighbors. They didn't move in the same circles. Which is to say, Cross was respectable, and *he* was not.

"What time will she return?" Good Lord, was he

whining? Because it sounded very much as if he was whining.

"Not until this evening, I should think, my lord."

This evening! But it was only ten o'clock in the morning! The evening was *hours* away.

"Is there something I might do for you, Lord Hawke? Of course, Abby's here, as well, and we have an additional housemaid in from the village for the day, to make up for Miss Templeton's absence."

He stifled a snort. There wasn't a bloody housemaid in existence who could replace Helena Templeton. He didn't say so, of course, mainly because Mrs. Norris was already eyeing him as if he'd lost his wits. "No, not a thing, only who's to mind the boys today?"

"Not to worry, my lord. Miss Templeton arranges for them to be kept busy with lessons on her day off. They're engaged with their fencing master at the moment, and later this afternoon they'll go out with their riding master."

Riding master? How the devil had she managed that? "But the boys don't have horses."

"No, but Miss Templeton found a riding master in Steeple Barton who's willing to lend his horses. He has a pair of delightful roan ponies he brings for Ryan and Etienne."

Of course, because there wasn't a single thing Helena Templeton couldn't do. A wave of some emotion rolled over him at the thought of her searching out riding masters, but it wasn't *affection*, no matter how much it might feel like it. Earls didn't feel affection for their sons' governess. It was unseemly.

"Perhaps you'd like to ride out with the boys this afternoon, Lord Hawke? I'm certain your horse wants exercising. Ryan and Etienne would be thrilled to have you, and really, my lord, it's the dearest thing imaginable, to see them trotting about on their matching ponies." Mrs. Norris cast a shrewd look at him. "I daresay Miss Templeton will be vastly pleased to find you'd all been out together."

It was frightening, really, how adroitly Mrs. Norris managed him. "Perhaps I will." There was only so much time he could spend with Hecate, after all.

But until then, there was nothing for him to do but return to his study, stare into the fire, and do his best not to think about the plush softness of Helena Templeton's lower lip beneath his fingertips, and try not to count how many hours must elapse before evening arrived, and she'd return to Hawke's Run.

"YOU SEEM OUT OF SORTS, HELENA. ARE YOU QUITE ALL right, dearest?"

Helena startled, guilty heat rising in her cheeks as she jerked her attention back to Juliet, who was regarding her with an anxious frown on her pretty face. "I beg your pardon, Juliet. I'm perfectly well, just a bit distracted."

Juliet's frown deepened. "It's not the boys, is it?"

Dear Juliet. She was nearly as fond of Ryan and Etienne as Helena was. She never failed to ask about them ever since she'd met them several months ago, after she'd fled a house party at Steeple Cross, arrived unexpectedly at Hawke's Run early in morning and promptly burst into a flood of tears over some business having to do with Lord Cross.

Helena had never quite worked out what had

gone awry between them, but Lord Cross had appeared that evening in a rather startling scarlet waistcoat, shouted verses of Shakespeare up at Juliet from underneath a bedchamber window, and four weeks later, Juliet had married him.

It was a curious business, but to see them now, one would never believe anything but the most ardent love could ever have existed between Lord and Lady Cross. They were utterly devoted to each other.

"No, the boys are fine, it's just that Lord Hawke returned home rather suddenly last week, and things at Hawke's Run have been a bit unsettled since then."

"Lord Hawke's back from London?" Juliet's lovely blue eyes went wide. "My goodness. I confess I didn't anticipate that happening anytime soon. Lord Hawke is an, er...*eager* participant in the entertainments London has to offer."

"Entertainments, Juliet? By that, I take you to be referring to Lord Hawke's rumored wickedness?"

"Are they just rumors, then? Goodness knows I don't take a word that falls from the *ton*'s lips as sacred truth. For all I know, Lord Hawke is positively saintly."

"He's hardly saintly, I assure you. Some scandal or other drove him out of London." She'd expected Abby would have heard from her sister before now with a full accounting of the latest gossip regarding Lord Hawke, but as the days passed, whatever had landed him at Hawke's Run mattered less and less to her. "I can't say what it was, though, or whether or not it's true."

Juliet snorted. "Likely not, or at the very least it's not as bad as the gossips make it out to be. Does he realize you're one of the infamous Templeton sisters?"

"I don't think so, no. If he has heard the gossip about us, he hasn't yet connected it to me." Which was odd, really, given he'd just come from town, and half the *ton* was still buzzing about the wicked Templeton sisters who'd tricked two of London's most eligible earls into marriage with their clever matchmaking schemes.

Or so the *ton* would have it. Half the ladies in London wanted to scratch her sisters' eyes out. The other half wanted to know how they'd done it, so they might trap husbands of their own, but of course, there was no trick to it, no trap. Lord Melrose had fallen madly in love with Emmeline, and Lord Cross with Juliet.

It was simply love, and that was all.

"Well, it's lucky he hasn't figured out who you are, though he's likely to work it out at some point. What's he like?" Juliet leaned forward, her eyes dancing. "I do hope at least *some* of the rumors about him are true! He's said to be extraordinarily handsome, and extraordinarily wicked, and one does tend to be fascinated by a handsome, wicked earl, doesn't one?"

"He's..." Goodness, how did one even begin to describe Lord Hawke? "He's certainly one of those things," she muttered, more to herself than Juliet.

"For pity's sake, Helena, you're a dreadful tease!" Juliet set her teacup in the saucer. "Which one is it? Is he handsome, or wicked?"

"He isn't wicked." The *ton* might whisper all they liked about him, but nothing on earth could persuade her he was wicked. Confused, yes. Heartbroken, certainly.

But wicked? No. He wasn't that.

"Ah, he's as handsome as rumor says, then! But I'm surprised to hear you say he's not wicked, dearest, given what you've said of him in the past about his shameful neglect of his boys."

She had thought him shameful at one time, hadn't she? Shameful and selfish. Yet it seemed a long time ago that she'd believed that about him, despite his only having been at Hawke's Run for one week. Everything had changed so drastically since then! "That was when I believed he kept away because he preferred debauchery to fatherhood."

"That's not the case, then? I must say I'm relieved at it, Helena. One doesn't like to think of those naughty, wonderful boys without a proper father."

"No. His wife died, and I think...I think he was heartbroken, Juliet, and for a long while couldn't bear to be at Hawke's Run." This was pure speculation on her part, of course. She didn't know much about the late Lady Hawke, but since Lord Hawke's return, Mrs. Norris had made a few comments that indicated it was something of that nature.

"Oh, dear. That's terribly sad. Lady Hawke must have been quite young when she died."

"She was." Young and beautiful, if the portrait of her that hung in the gallery was an accurate representation. "Her death was sudden and unexpected. A fever, Mrs. Norris said."

Juliet sighed. "I see. I'm very sorry for Lord Hawke, then. Grief does make people behave unlike themselves, doesn't it?"

They were both quiet for a moment, and Helena knew they were each thinking of their own father, who'd passed away the previous year, after their mother had abandoned them all and fled to the Continent with her lover. She'd died there, and less than two years later their father had followed her to the grave, his heart broken. They'd lost him to his grief, and she couldn't bear to see the same thing happen to Ryan and Etienne.

"What sort of father is Lord Hawke?" Juliet asked. "I can't imagine he doesn't dote on those boys."

"He does, but he's cautious with them, and uncertain. He's been gone long enough that he no longer knows how to interact with them, but he *wants* to, Juliet." She met her sister's eyes. "He loves them very much, and they adore him."

"Well, one can't ask for more than that, can one? As long as they love each other, it can't help but come right in the end. Yet you still seem troubled, Helena. Is there something else?"

The truth was right there on the edge of her lips, and goodness knew if she could confide her troubles to anyone, it was Juliet. Yet still she hesitated. It was just...well, it was all just so ridiculous, like something out of a romantic novel.

How could she possibly look her sister in the eyes and admit that when she saw Lord Hawke making his lonely way across the frozen stable yard in the dark every morning her heart shuddered in her chest, as if it might break? How could she tell her sister his touch made her burn? Or describe the fierce love he had for his boys, and confess that it made her wish for that love for herself, and for things that could never be?

She was far too sensible a lady to imagine any good could ever come of such absurd fantasies. Lord Hawke was an *earl*. Her two elder sisters might be countesses now, but their marriages had been utter flukes, not to mention uproarious scandals. The *ton* still whispered that Emmeline and Juliet had fed their husbands some sort of magic love potion, for pity's sake. If anything, the Templetons were even more notorious now than they'd been before her sisters married.

Lord Hawke wasn't going to marry his sons' scandalous governess. Really, it was so entirely out of the question, there didn't seem much point in even mentioning it, so she swallowed the flood of words, and shook her head. "No, there's nothing, dearest. I just worry about the boys, as you know."

"I do know." Juliet was quiet for a while, seemingly lost in her own thoughts, but then she asked, "Do you suppose Lord Hawke intends to remain in Oxfordshire with his sons this time, or will he return to London?"

"I wish I knew. I think he wants to stay, but nothing's certain at this point."

"It would be just as well if he *did* stay." Juliet avoided Helena's eyes. "Now more than ever."

Helena raised an eyebrow at that cryptic comment. "What does *that* mean? Come, Juliet, what's the matter? You're acting strange."

"I suppose there's no sense putting it off any longer." Juliet let out a long sigh. "Dearest, there's something I must speak to you about, and...well, the truth is I've been dreading it, as I know it's going to upset you."

"What is it? It's not Euphemia or Tilly, is it?" Dread tightened Helena's throat. "It can't be Emmeline. I've just had a letter from her, and she seems very well—"

"No, it's nothing like that. No one's ill. At least, not physically."

"Just say it, Juliet! You know I can't bear this sort of waffling."

"Yes, all right. It *is* Euphemia. She's lonely, Helena. She doesn't say so," Juliet added, before Helena could speak, "But she is. One need only read between the lines of her letters to see it."

Helena abandoned her tea cake on her plate, her appetite gone. "Yes, I've noticed that as well. It must seem dreadfully quiet at home, with just Phee and Tilly there."

"Yes. I daresay five young ladies make a great deal more noise than two."

Yes, but it wasn't just that. Euphemia was the eldest, and she'd taken care of them all after their mother left. Phee's own romantic prospects had been shattered by their mother's scandal, so Phee had stepped into their mother's place. "It must seem to her as if we've all abandoned her," Helena murmured, a pang in her chest.

"I think it must, rather. She knows we haven't, of course, but what one knows logically and how one feels are not, alas, the same thing."

"No, they're not." Not at all. If she'd learned nothing else since Lord Hawke came to Hawke's Run, she'd learned that. "But I thought Phee agreed to spend more time here with you at Steeple Cross, and with Emmeline and Lord Melrose."

Juliet gave a helpless shrug. "I've tried to coax her to come here, Helena. Miles and I have done everything we can think of to lure her to Steeple Cross, and I know and Emmeline and Johnathan have done the same. We can't persuade her to leave Hambleden House."

"Not even for Tilly's sake?" Tilly was their youngest sister, and rather a wild little hellion. "Tilly won't be content to remain cooped up at home if she can be here, or with Emmeline in Kent."

"Yes, and I'm afraid that only makes it worse. As Tilly gets a glimpse of life beyond the tiny town of Hambleden, she'll want to leave more often, and Phee won't deny her. She'd never stand in the way of Tilly's happiness."

"Then Phee will be alone." Alone, in that rambling old place with the sloped floors and drafty windows, with nothing but her memories to keep her company. It was an unbearable fate for poor Phee, so awful it didn't bear thinking about.

Juliet reached for her hand, her gaze pleading. "Yes. Something must be done, Helena."

Only then did it dawn on her what Juliet was saying, what she was asking.

One of them would have to go home.

It couldn't be Emmeline or Juliet. They were both married now, with their homes and their husbands to think of, and children were sure to follow soon enough.

There was only one logical solution, only one of them who *could* go.

She was going to have to leave Hawke's Run.

CHAPTER
TEN

"Have you seen Lord Hawke yet this morning, Abby?" Helena paced from the stove to the kitchen table before finally giving up, dropping into a chair and resting her chin in her hands.

Was it really only nine o'clock in the morning? It felt as if years had passed since she'd left Steeple Cross yesterday evening.

"Nay, miss. I daresay his lordship is still in his bed." Abby sprinkled a dusting of flour over her pastry before attacking it with the rolling pin. "The quality likes to lie about in their beds till the afternoon, you know."

That made Helena smile, despite the heavy weight that had settled in her chest since her conversation with Juliet yesterday. If Abby knew how early Lord Hawke woke, and what he did in those dark morning hours, she'd faint dead away.

He'd been in his study when she returned to Hawke's Run yesterday evening. She'd noticed the light underneath the door, but she'd passed by without knocking. If she *had* knocked, he likely would have let her in, and then she would have been obliged to tell him she was leaving Hawke's Run.

Leaving the boys, and Mrs. Norris and Abby, and Hecate, Hestia and Poseidon.

Leaving him.

It would happen soon, too, just after Christmas. She and Juliet had decided it couldn't wait any longer than that, as Tilly was meant to spend several months of the new year in Kent with Emmeline and Lord Melrose.

She should have told him last night. It was pure foolishness for her to have fled upstairs without speaking to him, as if she were a child fleeing a scolding. It wouldn't do the least bit of good, pretending it wasn't happening. It wouldn't change anything.

But somehow, she simply couldn't make herself knock on his study door last night. It was too soon, her heart too raw still. She would surely have burst into tears as soon as she opened her mouth.

So, she'd run upstairs, and had woken this morning regretting her cowardice. It wasn't as if it were going to get easier if she put it off, and neither was it fair to Lord Hawke or the boys, as it would take time to secure a new governess...

A new governess. Someone else, someone name-less and faceless taking care of *her* boys, watching over *her* cats, laughing with *her* Abby, and bringing tea to her...her...

Her *nothing*. No one here belonged to her. This wasn't her home. Her home was with Phee and Tilly in Herefordshire, at Hambleden Manor.

"Are you ill, miss?" Abby's rolling pin paused mid-turn. "You look right miserable, you do."

"No, I'm fine, Abby." Helena pasted a smile on her

lips. "It's just that I wanted a word with Lord Hawke before the boys and I left for the Ladies Benevolent Society meeting this morning." They were due at St. Mary's soon, and it was a half hour's walk from Hawke's Run to the church.

"You could go and fetch him from his bed yourself, miss." Abby gave her a saucy wink. "Mind, you enter the bedchamber of a rake like Lord Hawke, you'll not come back out the same as you went in, if you take my meaning."

"Hush, Abby, you naughty thing."

Abby cackled. "Here, miss. You can take my rolling pin with you."

"Stop that." Helena batted the rolling pin away. "You shouldn't gossip as you do, Abby. It's terribly wicked of you."

"Is that so then, miss? Well, since gossip's so wicked, I suppose you don't want to hear what my sister wrote to me about Lord Hawke's scandal, do you?"

Did she? She no longer knew. It was a dreadful invasion of Lord Hawke' privacy, but it might prove useful for her to know, and anyway, there wasn't much chance of silencing Abby, who was clearly bursting to tell the tale. "So, there *is* a scandal, then?"

"Oh my, yes!" Abby glanced at the kitchen door, then leaned over the table, lowering her voice. "It's like this, miss. According to my sister, Lord Hawke is rumored to be having a torrid affair with...who do you think, miss? Just guess!"

A torrid affair? Well, of course, his scandal involved a beautiful, fashionable lady. Scandals always did. There was no reason that should make her heart sink, but there it went, right into her half-boots. "I haven't the faintest idea, Abby."

"You'd never guess it, anyway." Abby paused for effect, then announced rather breathlessly, "Why, it's none other than Lady Pamela Fielding!"

Lady Pamela Fielding? No doubt Lady Pamela Fielding was a very important personage, indeed, but the name meant nothing to Helena. "Who, pray tell, is Lady Pamela Fielding?"

"Why, she's Prinny's current mistress, of course." Abby threw her hands up in the air, exasperated. "Really, miss. Her name has been in the scandal sheets for weeks!"

"Is it just gossip, or do you suppose..." Helena swallowed the lump in her throat. "Do you suppose it's actually true?"

"As to that, I can't say, but Lord Hawke does run in the highest circles. He's wealthy and handsome, and all the ladies are in love with him. He's rumored to be so charming he can coax a snake from its skin." Abby cast a nervous glance at the door, then slid into the seat across from Helena's. "I daresay Lady Pamela sheds one lover for another more often than a snake does its skin, eh, miss?"

"That analogy doesn't quite work, Abby."

Abby waved this away. "That's not all, either. From what my sister tells me, Prinny nearly caught them out!"

"Caught them out?"

"Yes. It seems Prinny paid a late and unexpected visit to Lady Pamela, and when he entered her private apartments he heard a scuffle, and then he saw Lady Pamela push a gentleman out her window, and what do you think, miss?"

A sick feeling had settled in her stomach, but she'd come too far to stop now. "What?"

"Lord Hawke arrived here the very next day!" Abby drew herself up with an unmistakable air of triumph.

Helena slumped in her chair. That story would explain his missing boot and cravat, and his sudden appearance on Saturday morning, wouldn't it? "I suppose it must have been Lord Hawke hopping out Lady Pamela's window," she said dully.

"I daresay it was, but Lady Pamela's antics have come back to haunt her. My sister says Prinny's broken with her! He's said to be fed up with her nonsense, and now he's saying Lord Hawke can keep her, and welcome!"

"Keep her!" Oh, *no*. This was dreadful! If Prinny really had washed his hands of Lady Pamela and turned her over to Lord Hawke with his blessing, then there was no reason at all Lord Hawke couldn't return to London at once! As soon as he heard of it, he'd be off to town again, and then she'd be off to Herefordshire, and the boys would be left alone and heartbroken—

"My goodness, girls!" Mrs. Norris strode into the kitchen then, her brows drawn down in a frown. "What in heaven's name are the two of you shouting about? I can hear you clearly all the way from the entryway."

Not *too* clearly, hopefully. "I beg your pardon, Mrs. Norris. It's nothing at all, just...er, I just found out Abby's making my favorite current scones for tea, that's all."

"Scones? Oh, very well, then. You'd best hurry,

Miss Templeton. The boys are waiting for you in the entryway."

"Thank you, Mrs. Norris." She leapt up from the table and hurried up the stairs, her mind whirling. She had to come up with a way to keep Lord Hawke from leaving Hawke's Run. But how? There was no way to keep him from finding out that Lady Pamela was now his for the taking. One of his friends from London was sure to write to him about it.

"Good morning, Miss Templeton!" Etienne called from the top of the stairs. He came charging down them, his brother right behind him.

"We'd better hurry, Miss Templeton." Ryan seized her hand and tugged her toward the entryway. "We're to play tag in the churchyard with Freddy and Ian, and whoever gets there last has to hunt for the others first."

"Yes, alright. We'll go at once." She took each of the boys' hands in hers and was hurrying to the door when a deep voice behind her stopped her in her tracks.

"Wait, Miss Templeton."

She stilled, a shiver darting up her spine. Lord Hawke.

"I thought I'd come along with you this morning."

"You want to come with us?" She turned to face him, and nearly choked on her tongue. He was wearing a bottle-green coat that perfectly matched his eyes, and fitted breeches that perfectly flattered his—

"Only if it's agreeable to you, Miss Templeton."

"Why, of course, but you do realize we're going to the St. Mary's Ladies' Benevolent Society Meeting?" It didn't seem at all the sort of thing that would interest him.

"Yes. I feel I must attend, Miss Templeton, to make certain my mistletoe is properly accounted for."

He gave her an uncertain little smile that melted her heart, and before she could stop herself, she was smiling back. "You're very welcome to accompany us, Lord Hawke."

"Hurrah!" Ryan cried, before darting out the door, Etienne chasing after him.

"I was surprised to find the boys attend the St. Mary's Ladies' Benevolent Society meetings with you, Miss Templeton," Lord Hawke began, as they made their way down the well-worn path that led to the village of Steeple Barton. "I've no idea how you talked them into *that*."

"Oh, they don't come inside, but chase around with the other boys in the churchyard. I've gotten into the habit of taking them with me everywhere, my lord, though I confess there are days when it would be easier to simply lock them in a cupboard until I return from my errands."

He laughed. "You could leave them with Abby, or Mrs. Norris."

"I suppose, but they're busy, and besides, I enjoy the boys' company very much. I'd never choose to leave them behind," she added, her smile fading.

"Well, let's hope you never have to."

It was the perfect opening, the ideal moment to tell him she *would* have to leave them, and soon, but she couldn't make the words leave her lips. Not now, on such a beautiful morning, with the sky a brilliant blue above them, the boys' lively chatter carrying on the clear, bright air, and Lord Hawke walking beside her, the breeze ruffling his dark hair.

It wasn't difficult to see why Lady Pamela would prefer Lord Hawke to the plump Prince Regent, for all that he was destined to become king. Lord Hawke was wonderfully tall, and, er...firm, in all the places a gentleman was meant to be firm, and he had the loveliest green eyes imaginable, the same dark green as forest ferns.

What would become of him, if he returned to London now, and took up with that awful Lady Pamela again? Because of course, she *must* be awful— and spent every night overindulging in brandy and debauchery?

He was a strong, strapping man, but how much abuse could any man's body endure? If something happened to him, what would become of the boys? They'd be left parentless, and—

"Good day, Miss Templeton!"

The cheerful voice tore her from her musings, and she looked up in surprise to find they'd reached the churchyard, and Lady Goodall and her niece Lady Anne were waiting at the entrance to the church.

"Hullo, Freddy!" Ryan shouted, waving at his friend.

"Don't shout, if you please, Ryan."

"Beg pardon, Miss Templeton. Can't we go and play now?" Etienne turned to her with a pleading look. "Freddy and Ian are waiting for us!"

"Yes, go on. I'll fetch you when we're finished."

The boys raced off, and Helena hurried forward to take Lady Goodall's outstretched hand. "Lady Goodall, and Lady Anne. How do you do? Oh, dear. Is something amiss? You look rather grim, my lady."

"Yes, I'm afraid a rather significant impediment has arisen in our plans, but my goodness, is this truly Lord Hawke I see before me? I can scarcely believe my eyes!"

If the comment had come from anyone other than Lady Goodall it might have sounded like a reprimand, but she was all kindness and graciousness, and the smile she offered Lord Hawke was sweetness itself.

"Lady Goodall. It's a pleasure to see you again." Lord Hawke bowed over Lady Goodall's hand, then straightened again, a smile on his lips that utterly transformed his face.

Helena stared at him. This wasn't the surly Lord Hawke that had helped free her from the tree, or the distant Lord Hawke who regarded his sons with a strange sort of detached confusion, as if he'd never laid eyes on them before, nor was it the angry Lord Hawke who'd shouted at her after that fiasco on the staircase.

This was a Lord Hawke she'd only ever had the briefest glimpse of before, the Lord Hawke who lurked beneath the unhappy man she'd encountered on the drive a week ago. Perhaps he didn't realize it yet, but Hawke's Run was good for him. He was happy here.

"You remember my niece, of course, my." Lady Goodall drew Lady Anne forward.

"Of course. I believe she pushed me into the pond once when we were children." He bowed over Lady Anne's dainty hand. "How do you do, my lady?"

"As I remember it, I pushed you into the pond because you threw a fish at me, and dirtied my new blue frock."

He laughed. "Dreadful! I'm surprised you didn't drown me."

"Never. It's lovely to see you, Lord Hawke." Lady Anne smiled, her cheeks flushing a becoming pink.

"Indeed, my lord, it truly is wonderful to see you in Steeple Barton again. I do hope you intend to stay for a while? Oh, and I must congratulate you on finding such an excellent governess for your sons! We think the world of Miss Templeton, do we not, Anne?"

Lady Anne gave Helena a warm smile. "Indeed, we do, Aunt."

"Well, we'd best go inside, hadn't we? We have rather a lot to discuss today." Lady Goodall took Lord Hawke's arm, and he escorted her inside.

"My goodness, Lord Hawke is a handsome gentleman, isn't he?" Lady Anne took Helena's arm, her pretty face alight with interest. "It's been ages since I've seen him. Does he not come to church on Sundays?"

Lady Anne wasn't one who listened to *ton* gossip, it seemed. "He only just arrived at Hawke's Run from London last week, my lady."

"Oh. Well, it's lovely of him to take an interest in the Ladies' Benevolent Society's doings. Not many gentlemen do, I'm afraid."

"No. I confess I'm quite surprised he came this morning." It was the very last thing she would have expected of him, but it wasn't the first time he'd surprised her, was it?

Nearly every lady in Steeple Barton was a member of the Benevolent Society, so the anteroom to one side of the chapel was crowded with nearly two dozen women, all of them chattering at once. Lady Codswaddle was holding forth on some topic or other, as she tended to do, while poor Miss Fanning scurried about, trying to find chairs for everyone.

But when Lord Hawke walked in with Lady Goodall, every head turned in their direction, and little by little the chatter ceased, and the room plunged into silence. Some of the ladies merely stared at him curiously, but some appeared to recognize him, and began whispering to each other.

Lady Goodall didn't pay any mind to them, but gave Lord Hawke's arm a little pat, and took her place at the head of the room. "Good afternoon, ladies. Christmas day draws near, and we've a good deal to accomplish still if we're to turn a tidy profit for the St. Mary's Poor Fund. Before we begin, however, I must—"

"What's to be done about the Christmas pies, my lady?" Lady Codswaddle's nasal voice rose about the chatter. "Mrs. Holcroft always makes them, but she's been called away to her daughter in Tidmington, and I don't see how we're to have a Christmas fete without Christmas pies."

"My dear Lady Codswaddle, there's no need to fret. The Christmas pie crisis will be addressed, I assure you, but we've a more pressing problem to deal with first."

"I can't think what could be more pressing than Christmas pies." Lady Codswaddle drew herself up with an important sniff. "Why, it's not Christmas at all without—"

"The ballroom at Goodall Abbey has flooded," Lady Goodall interrupted. "I'm very sorry for it, ladies, but the floors were destroyed, and they'll all have to be torn out. It's going to take months, and that means the Christmas fete can't be held at Goodall Abbey."

A gasp went up.

"Not be held at Goodall Abbey! But the St. Mary's Ladies' Benevolent Society's Annual Christmas Fete always takes place at Goodall Abbey!" Lady Codswaddle shrieked. "It's *tradition*."

"I'm aware of that, but there's nothing to be done." Lady Goodall gave a helpless shrug. "We'll simply have to find another place this year."

"There *isn't* any other place! Goodall Abbey is the only residence with a ballroom large enough to accommodate us! Oh dear, oh dear, this is dreadful, indeed!" Lady Codswaddle fumbled in her reticule for a handkerchief and pressed it to her eyes. "We'll have to cancel the fete!"

"Cancel it! We can't cancel it!" Miss Fanning wailed. "What's to become of the Poor Fund if we cancel it?"

"Well, the poor will simply have to manage for themselves, won't they?" Lady Codswaddle snapped. "The fete is only five days away! We'll never find a place on such short notice."

Miss Fanning began to cry then, and Lady Codswaddle to scold, and every voice in the anteroom rose to a fever pitch, half the ladies shouting out suggestions while the other half shook their heads and pronounced the fete finished, for certain.

Helena didn't say a word.

She sat quietly in the midst of the chaos, turning an idea over in her mind.

Could it work? She'd have to set it in motion quickly, right this minute, and Lord Hawke was likely to be utterly furious with her, but then, what was the worst that could happen? He'd be angry, yes, but it would keep him here for a few more days, at least.

A great deal could happen in five days.

It would be an excellent way to draw him back into the community, as well. Perhaps by the end of it the lure of London and that dreadful Lady Pamela would fade, and he'd make up his mind to stay at Hawke's Run for good.

It would be a great deal of fuss and bother, of course, but if she could see the thing done, it would help everyone. Surely, he'd recognize that, once he got over his pique?

She rose to her feet, her mind made up. "I beg your pardon, Lady Goodall, but Goodall Abbey's ballroom *isn't* the only place in Steeple Barton large enough to accommodate the fete."

"Ladies, ladies!" Lady Goodall rapped her cane on the floor to get everyone's attention. "For pity's sake, I can't hear myself think! Do endeavor to remember that you are in fact ladies, if you please. Now, Miss Templeton, did you have something you wished to say?"

"Yes, thank you, my lady. I merely wish to point out that the ballroom at Hawke's Run's is quite large enough to fit all the residents of Steeple Barton, and the surrounding area besides."

"Hawke's Run!" Lord Hawke shot to his feet. "You can't mean to suggest—"

"Indeed, I do, my lord." Helena turned her most ingratiating smile on the surrounding ladies. "I move that the St. Mary's Ladies' Benevolent Society Christmas Fete be held at Hawke's Run this year."

ELEVEN

Adrian wasn't a lady, nor was he particularly benevolent, yet somehow, he'd just become the newest and most generous member of the St. Mary's Ladies' Benevolent Society.

Helena Templeton might look innocent, with those wide blue-gray eyes, but she was as wily as a fox. Hers wasn't the first trap that had ever been laid for him, of course. Lady Pamela's failed attempts to lure him into her bed came to mind, but her ladyship's wits were, alas, no match for Miss Templeton's. *Her* trap was so subtle, so diabolically clever the steel teeth of the thing had snapped closed before he even realized he'd stepped into it.

"It's dreadfully unfair of us to impose on you at such a late date, Lord Hawke, but if you *could* see you way clear to hosting the fete at Hawke's Run this year, we'd be ever so grateful to you." Lady Goodall gave him a hopeful smile.

"Oh, my lord, it would be ever so good of you!" Miss Fanning breathed, her hands clasped under her chin, her tear-streaked face pleading. "It *is* for the poor, you know."

There was no way out, was there? No, the steel teeth were tightening around his leg with each moment that passed. He was surrounded on every side by Steeple Barton's godliest ladies, all of them holding their collective breaths, their faces bright with expectation. Unless he wished to be known as the man who turned his back on Steeple Barton's wretched poor—at *Christmas*, no less—then he hadn't any choice but to invite the good ladies of the St. Mary's Benevolent Society to flood Hawke's Run with Christmas pies and kissing balls.

He *should* be furious with Helena over this. His jaw should be clenched, his extremities rigid, his entire person seething with outrage at such a trick, but all he could manage was a dazed sort of admiration for her.

Good Lord, he was a fool, but even her tricks charmed him.

The thing was as good as done now, in any case, and there was nothing for it but to submit with the graciousness that became an earl. So, he turned his most engaging smile on the assembled ladies and swept into a deep bow. "Ladies, you do me a great honor, permitting me to serve Steeple Barton in such a pleasurable manner. Hawke's Run is at your disposal."

The delighted squeals and explosion of excited feminine chatter would surely have sent him home with his head ringing if Lady Goodall hadn't stepped forward and held up her hand for silence. "Now, ladies, of course we're all extremely grateful to Lord Hawke for his generosity—really, my lord, you've quite saved the day—but we've rather a lot to accomplish still if we're to see this thing done properly, so let's get back to it, shall we?"

The ladies scurried back to their places and the meeting went on, with Lady Goodall droning on about something to do with Hawke's Run and an emergency meeting of the decorations committee, but she went on at such tedious length about wreaths and candlelight and kissing balls he gave up, and let his attention wander.

There was no need for *him* to listen, after all. He didn't know a damned thing about wreaths or kissing balls, and God knew there'd be no shortage of ladies about to tell him what to do.

Instead, his attention wandered to Helena, who was seated in the chair directly in front of him. If he looked closely, he could just glimpse a sliver of her white neck between the edge of her sensible bun and the collar of her drab gray dress.

It was a lovely neck, it must be said, long and graceful, though one had to gaze at her rather intently to notice it, so effectively had she hidden it underneath her tightly-bound hair and severe gown.

So, he gazed—and gazed, and gazed—until a flush stained that delicate skin, and she pressed a self-conscious hand there, as if she could feel the heat of his eyes on her, and dear God, he wanted to touch her, trace that wash of pink with his fingertips and his tongue, then pull those wretched pins from her hair one by one so the heavy locks fell over her shoulders as they'd done that dark morning she'd gone in search of Hestia and found *him* as well, the wayward golden-brown curls tickling her neck, and...

Ahem. Church was hardly the proper place for such heated fantasies, and his breeches were growing uncomfortably tight, so he tore his gaze away from that tempting sliver of skin, cursing silently to himself as the meeting went on and on, mainly due to Lady Codswaddle, who seemed to love nothing so much as the sound of her own voice.

Finally, when he was ready to tear his hair out by the roots, it came to an end, and the ladies began to disperse. Helena jumped to her feet and darted for the door without so much as a glance in his direction, but he let her go, following along at a leisurely pace.

They both knew he'd catch her eventually—

"Lord Hawke? Might I have a word?"

Lady Anne was hurrying across the room toward him, and he paused at the doorway to wait for her. "Of course, my lady. How can I help?"

"Oh, but you've already done so, my lord!" She came to a breathless stop beside him. "I couldn't let you go without thanking you once again for your generosity in loaning Hawke's Run for the fete. My poor aunt has been beside herself all week, certain we'd have to cancel it, but you've arrived home just in time to save us, it seems."

"It's my pleasure." He offered her his arm.

She took it, smiling up at him. "Yes, well, we'll see if you're still pleased once the decorating committee descends on you. Permit me to offer my most sincere apologies for Lady Codswaddle in advance, Lord Hawke."

He laughed, and escorted her outdoors. They waited by the entryway, chatting amiably until Lady Goodall, having finally escaped Lady Codswaddle's clutches, came to fetch Lady Anne and take her home.

By the time he'd handed them into their carriage and reached the churchyard, Helena was already gathering up the boys. "Come, Ryan and Etienne. It's time to resume your lessons."

"Aw, but Miss Templeton!" Etienne's lower lip poked out. "We've hardly had a chance to play yet!"

Adrian raised an eyebrow at that. Hardly a chance? Surely, they'd been trapped inside that church with Lady Codswaddle for the better part of the last century?

"At once, if you please, gentlemen," Helena called, waving them over.

That was all. She didn't bargain, or plead, or even scold, only issued that one calm command, and the boys fell into line at once, albeit reluctantly. "Alright, but can we race, Miss Templeton?" Ryan begged. "Etienne told Freddy and Ian he runs faster than me, but he doesn't, and I'll prove it, too!"

She cast a sidelong glance at him, her lower lip trapped between her teeth, but the inevitable reckoning was upon her. She knew it well, and let out a sigh. "Yes, alright, but don't go so far ahead we can no longer see you, if you please."

"We won't!" Ryan tore off with Etienne right after him.

Adrian bided his time, holding his tongue, and they walked for some time in silence until he began to fear for the wellbeing of her abused lower lip, and cleared his throat. "That was quite a clever scheme, Miss Templeton. I never even saw it coming. Bravo."

"It wasn't a scheme at all, my lord, merely a suggestion!" He raised an eyebrow at that, and a guilty flush flooded her cheeks. "You might have refused, if you wished to."

"What, and have every benevolent lady in Steeple Barton cursing my name? No, indeed. I daresay it wouldn't be the first time Lady Codswaddle has called curses down on a man's head."

He angled his face closer to hers, hoping to catch her gaze, and was rewarded by a glimpse of blue-gray eyes and the quirk of a red lip. "You surprise me, my lord."

"Do I? I don't see why." Though it was only fair if he *did* surprise her, given she'd been turning him inside out since she'd thrown that bunch of mistletoe in his face.

"It's just...does it matter to you, what the people of Steeple Barton think of you?"

"Of course, it does." The words tumbled out before he'd even considered them, but it was the truth, wasn't it? Prior to his return to Hawke's Run, he might have said he *didn't* give a bloody damn what the fine citizens of this village thought of him, but then he hadn't given a damn about much of anything then, had he?

It was different now.

He'd spent some of the happiest years of his life here. Perhaps he could be happy here again, someday. "This is my country seat, Miss Templeton. My family has lived in Steeple Barton for generations, and I'm well aware of my obligations to the people here."

"Of course, Lord Hawke. I beg your pardon. I meant no offense. I think it's a lovely place, myself." She gave him a shy smile. "Ryan and Etienne seem happy here."

"Yes." He glanced at the boys, who were some yards ahead, sliding over the patches of ice as they raced home. Their wild shrieks of laughter split the air, and his throat tightened. "Yes, I think they are."

They didn't speak again until the pathway let out

into the stable yard at Hawke's Run. Ryan and Etienne were there, waiting outside the stable door. "Ah. It must be time for feline husbandry."

"*Feline* husbandry!" She let out a surprised laugh. "Is that what you call it?"

"Er, well...perhaps I do, but only to myself, and occasionally to that trying feline you have penned up in the stables."

"Trying? What's she done?"

"She's a greedy little opportunist, that's what. She refuses to have a thing to do with me unless I bring her treats."

"Oh, dear. That *is* a sad failing, isn't it?"

She was doing her best to look serious, but he had no trouble reading the look in her eyes. Amusement. She was *laughing* at him. "I don't believe you think it's sad at all, Miss Templeton. I think you find it all quite entertaining."

"It's just that I can't help but wonder, my lord, why a man with such a virulent hatred of felines would visit the stables every morning to check on a cat he surely despises, and bring her treats in the first place."

"I didn't do it for the cat—"

"Hecate. Her name is Hecate."

"Very well, then. I didn't do it for Hecate." Though if he ever *were* going to befriend a cat, it would be that one. She was a greedy opportunist, just as he'd said, but he couldn't help but admire the creature's pluck.

"Ah. Who, then?"

"The boys."

She already knew it, of course. She'd guessed it days ago, but naturally she wouldn't rest until she'd made him confess everything to her. If ever there was a lady for poking about in things that didn't concern her, it was this one. "They seem fond of her, and they'll be heartbroken if anything happens to her, so I'm making sure nothing does."

"But that's lovely, Lord Hawke. I don't know why you'd want to make a secret of it."

It was a simple question, but the answer was complicated. So much so that even he wasn't sure he understood it all, so he said nothing.

"You will join us for feline husbandry today, won't you, Lord Hawke? Just think, Hecate could be giving birth at this very moment. You wouldn't want to miss it, would you?"

"Nonsense. It's only the fifty-seventh day of Hecate's gestational cycle. According to your charts, she's still six days shy of the period she's most likely to give birth."

Her jaw dropped open. "You consulted the charts?"

"I might have glanced at it."

She raised an eyebrow, and he blew out a breath. "Oh, very well, I consulted the charts, but only because they were right there, pinned to the stable wall. I wonder who put them there?" He reached around her and opened the stable door with a tug. "Come on, then. If we're going to go, let's go."

She followed him, rubbing her hands together. "I do hope Hecate wasn't cold last night. It was quite bitter when I came out this morning, and remains so, despite the sunshine."

"She wasn't cold, I assure you." He sighed. Was a man permitted no secrets? "Hecate has my coat. I wrapped it around her before I went to bed last night."

She laughed again, and he turned to gaze at her as the sweet sound echoed in the frosty morning, warming him from the inside out. She had a lovely laugh, bright and joyous. It was the sort of laugh that lured a smile to the face of anyone who happened to be near her, the sort of laugh one wanted to hear again and again.

"It's just as well you're coming in today, my lord. I daresay Hecate would be dreadfully put out if she discovered you'd passed by the stables without paying homage to her."

"I wouldn't dream of disappointing Hecate." He'd missed feline husbandry lessons yesterday, and he wouldn't make that mistake again. "Lead on, Miss Templeton."

"We'll have to hurry through it, I'm afraid," she was saying as they joined the boys by the pen. "It's only a few hours until the decorating committee arrives, and the boys still need their luncheon—"

"The decorating committee! What, are they coming here *today*?"

"Why, yes, this afternoon. You agreed to it at the meeting just now." She turned to face him, her lips twitching. "Oh, dear. You weren't listening to a word Lady Goodall said, were you?"

"Not as attentively as I should have been, it seems." Fortunately, just as he'd expected, there was no shortage of ladies eager to tell him what to do.

By the time Hawke's Run's iron-studded doors closed behind the ladies of the Benevolent Society's decorating committee later that evening, Adrian's ears were ringing, and his fingers ached from the effort it had taken not to wring Lady Codswaddle's neck.

Lady Anne had tried to warn him.

It was astonishing, the unrelenting chaos a mere dozen ladies could cause. They'd poked their inquisitive little noses into every nook and cranny of the castle. Not a single corner from the entryway to the ballroom escaped their notice, and from the discussions he'd overheard, every inch of it was doomed to be draped with holiday finery. How they'd produce enough ribbons and baubles to blanket every inch of Hawke's Run he couldn't say, but he'd wager his one remaining Hessian boot they'd find a way.

The afternoon had gone on far longer than any of them had anticipated it would. Ryan and Etienne had fled as soon as they saw the contingent of ladies bearing down on them, and had long since had their tea and escaped to their bedchamber.

He wanted nothing more than to do the same, but before he could drag himself up the stairs, order that a bath and a tray be brought to his room and spend the rest of the evening recovering from the assault on his senses, he had one small matter to see to first.

A small matter with red lips, blue-gray eyes, and a laugh like Christmas itself.

He hadn't seen Helena all afternoon, not since the sea of ladies had arrived and overflowed the entryway, all of them talking at once. Lady Goodall had asked him to take Lady Anne throughout the house soon after that, and he hadn't laid eyes on Helena since.

"Have you seen Miss Templeton anywhere, Mrs. Norris?"

Mrs. Norris was no stranger to the ladies of the Benevolent Society. She'd wrangled them before, but no one could have predicted the horror of a dozen of them here at once. His poor housekeeper looked as if she'd been trampled by a herd of cattle. "Miss Templeton? Let me think. I saw her several hours ago. Lady Codswaddle cornered her in the stairwell, and was going on and on about something to do with the kissing balls. Poor Miss Templeton appeared a bit frayed around the edges."

No doubt. Lady Codswaddle was enough to fray anyone's edges. Helena had volunteered them for this misadventure, yes, but an afternoon with Lady Codswaddle bellowing in her ear was punishment enough. "You didn't see her again after that?"

Mrs. Norris frowned. "Now you ask, I haven't laid eyes on her since. How strange. It's not at all like Miss Templeton to call that horde down upon our heads and then disappear in the midst of the torment. Perhaps I'd better go and—"

"No, it's alright, Mrs. Norris. I'll go find her." She couldn't have gotten far.

Mrs. Norris breathed out a sigh of relief. "If you're quite sure, my lord, then I'll go and see to Cook. One of the ladies made a rather rude comment about her curd tarts, and Cook didn't take it well."

He could guess which lady *that* had been. "I'm sure. Not to worry, Mrs. Norris."

A quick turn about the ground floor didn't turn up Helena. She wasn't in the kitchens, the breakfast parlor or the dining room. He peeked into the boys' bedchamber and found Ryan and Etienne there, fast asleep with their coverlets tucked under their chins, but there was no sign of Helena, and a knock on her bedchamber door went unanswered.

Where could she have gone to? Had she been shut in somewhere by accident? Perhaps Lady Codswaddle had kidnapped her. For a lady who was meant to be benevolent, that woman was a frightening old harridan.

He wandered back down the stairs, an uncomfortable twinge in his chest. It wasn't *worry*, precisely. Helena was perfectly able to take care of herself. He'd have felt the same twinge if anyone in his household had disappeared so thoroughly—

Wait. The stables! Of course. She'd been fretting about the cold earlier. She must have slipped outside to check on Hecate.

He made his way from the entryway to the staircase that led to the kitchens, but just as he was about to head down the pathway, he spotted a dim light peeking out from a crack in the stillroom door.

He crept toward it and pushed it open.

There was Miss Templeton, hunched over the long wooden table, her hair falling out of its tidy bun, a mass of what looked like thorny branches spread out before her, a single lantern shedding a dim circle of light over her work surface. She was fussing with something in her hands and muttering crossly to herself. "Six dozen! Seventy-two of the cursed things. I'll have to go up the alder tree again—"

"What in God's name are you *doing* down here?"

She jumped, a shriek falling from her lips, the little bundle in her hands sailing into the air as the stool she was sitting upon tipped backwards.

"Helena!" He caught her before she could topple

over, and for one delirious instant she was in his arms, the slender curve of her back pressed to his chest, her hair tickling his chin.

She's your sons' governess, your sons' governess...

He held her against him for a heartbeat, breathing in her scent, then set her firmly away from him before he forgot he was a gentleman, and leaned down to pick up the bundle she'd dropped.

"What's this?" He held it closer to the lamp and inspected it, but he couldn't make any sense of it. It looked like a haphazard collection of sticks and leaves, with a wrinkled bit of white ribbon tied in a straggling bow around it.

"What do you mean, what is it?" She glared at him. "It's a kissing ball! Can't you tell?"

"Er, well, I don't know that I've ever seen a kissing—"

That was as far as he got. She snatched the ball out of his hand, threw it aside, then folded her arms on the table, rested her head upon them, and burst into tears.

CHAPTER
TWELVE

S he was sobbing in front of Lord Hawke. Not just a few pretty, crystalline tears that glittered like dewdrops in her eyes, or even a restrained, dainty weeping, but sobbing, with all the ugliness such a state entailed.

Red face. Running nose. Puffy eyes. Mouth wide open, and great hoarse, sniveling sobs wrenched from her heaving chest and spewing from her contorted lips.

Sniveling. She was *sniveling* in front of Lord Hawke. Dear God, if she could have ducked under the table without his seeing it, she would have done so in an instant.

Or...was there any chance he hadn't noticed she was sobbing? Gentlemen weren't usually observant of such things, were they? Perhaps he didn't realize—

"Miss Templeton? I'm afraid you're, er...distressed."

Dash it, he *had* noticed.

"What's happened?" He gave her shoulder a gentle shake. "Why are you crying?"

Why? It was a perfectly reasonable question.

What she would have given in that moment to have uttered a perfectly reasonable answer in response! It was a great pity, then, that she hadn't the vaguest idea.

She was crying over nothing. And everything.

Lady Codswaddle had shouted at her. The fete was only four days away, and there was so much to do between now and then her head felt dizzy just thinking about it. She was exhausted, and...and...

And Lord Hawke—*Adrian*—had hardly spared her a glance all afternoon, because he'd been taken up with escorting Lady Anne into every room in the entire castle.

Even *she* hadn't seen every room in this castle!

They looked well together, he and Lady Anne. His dark hair and height complimented Lady Anne's fair daintiness, and then they were so easy with each other, laughing and chatting together as if no one else was in the room with them, as if no one else mattered, and...and...

She was being made to leave Hawke's Run, to abandon her sweet boys, and...and other people! The end of the year was creeping closer with every sunrise, and Ryan and Etienne were sure to forget her as soon as she'd gone, and she'd never get to see Hecate's kittens, and Abby would become a dreadful gossip, and poor Mrs. Norris would be run ragged trying to keep up with the boys, and Lord Hawke would fall madly in love Lady Anne, and everything was wretched—

"Please stop crying, Helena, and tell me what's wrong."

Helena? Had he just called her by her given name? That and the gentle hand he laid on her shoulder so startled her she swallowed her sobs and raised her head.

She blinked up at him, squinted, then blinked again.

His brows were pulled together, his lips turned down at the corners, and his hair was standing on end. He looked handsome and disheveled and perfectly miserable.

Even more miserable than she felt.

"I'm very sorry I shouted at you, and laughed at your..." He retrieved the pathetic little bundle of sticks and ribbons she'd tied together. "Your, ah...your kissing ball. It's a very nice one, indeed, and—"

"No, it isn't. It's awful." She took it from his hand with a sigh and tossed it onto the table. "And you didn't shout at me."

"I daresay it sounded like a shout to you, with the stillroom so quiet. I do beg your pardon for startling you." He gazed down at her in the dim light, his eyes soft and darker than usual, his pupils having swallowed all but the narrowest ring of forest green.

"I own you *did* startle me a bit." So much so her heart was thrashing like a wild thing against her rib cage. From the startling, that is. No other reason. "I thought everyone would have gone off to their beds by now."

"The boys are asleep, but Mrs. Norris was worried about you. She said she hadn't seen you in hours, and asked me to come look for you." He nodded at the mess spread out on the work table. "Can't this wait until tomorrow?"

"No, I'm afraid not." She let out a weary sigh. "Lady Codswaddle was a bit, er, dismayed to find I'd only made two dozen kissing balls." Dismayed, indeed. That was a polite word for what had, in fact, been an ill-tempered rant on Lady Codswaddle's part.

He frowned. "You mean to say you've been down here making kissing balls this entire time?"

"I'm afraid so. Hawke's Run's ballroom is much larger than Goodall Abbey's, you see, and so it's going to take far more kissing balls than we originally planned."

His lips had pulled into a thin, grim line. "How many more?"

She glanced at the enormous pile of greenery on the table and the overflowing basket of white silk ribbon, and allowed herself a despairing little sniffle. "Another six dozen."

"Six dozen! You mean to say Lady Codswallop is demanding you—"

"Codswaddle." She brushed a stray lock of hair from her damp face. Dash it, she was all drippy—

"My God, what happened to your hands?" He seized one of her wrists and brought her hand closer to the lantern light. "You're bleeding!"

"Only a little. It's nothing, I assure you."

She tugged gently to free her hand from his grasp, but he held on, turning it this way and that. Dozens of tiny cuts and pricks marred her skin, some of them oozing droplets of blood. "It's not nothing."

"The holly leaves are a bit pointy, that's all."

"Pointy? Your hands are torn to bits, Helena. It looks as if you've been mauled by all six of Circe's kittens."

Her jaw dropped. "Circe's kittens! You mean to say you *know* about them?"

"Do I know about Hestia, Poseidon, Artemis, Apollo, Demeter and Hephaestus? Of course, I do.

Even the wily Miss Templeton can't keep six kittens hidden. I kept seeing furry little tails darting around corners, so I asked the boys. They told me all about Circe, and gave me the kittens' names. Demeter and Artemis have been sleeping on a settee in my bedchamber for days."

She gaped up at him, her mouth wide open. *Again*. "But you despise cats!"

"I do. They're arrogant, hissing, self-satisfied little beasts." He turned her hand over to inspect her palms. They weren't quite as bad as the backs, but they were covered with scratches and punctures as well, and her fingers were a mess of slivers and smeared blood. "For God's sake, Lady Codswaddle expects you to make another *sixty* kissing balls? There will be nothing left of your hands but bloody stumps!"

"Thank you for that colorful description, my lord."

"That woman is an outrageous tyrant, and she's set you an impossible task. Tell her she can make do with the kissing balls she has, and be done with it."

"Oh, no. I can't do that, my lord."

He raised an eyebrow. "I can't think of a single reason why not."

"Because I'm on the decorations committee, and Lady Codswaddle is the head of it, and because I said I'd do the kissing balls."

"Twenty-four of them, yes. Not ninety-six. Lady Codswaddle has changed the rules."

"Yes, but I said I'd do it. I can't go back on my word now." No matter if she did end up with bloody stumps where her hands used to be.

"Even if your fingers fall off in the process?"

"I daresay it won't come to loss of limb, my lord. It's not as bad as that."

"Bad enough." He sighed and released her hand —which he'd been somehow inexplicably still holding—and turned to rummage through the cabinets behind him. "Mrs. Norris makes a peppermint salve for cuts. It's here somewhere, and the bandages—"

"There in the next cabinet to the right, on the top shelf."

"Here it is." He set the salve and bandages down on the table and reached for her. "Give me your hand."

She did as he bid her, the light stroke of his fingertips against her palm sending a shiver up her spine. He doused a bit of cotton cloth with the salve and began dabbing it on her cuts, his touch gentle, talking as he worked. "Can the boys be trusted to help you with the kissing balls?"

"Certainly, for short periods at a time, until they lose interest. Little boys aren't enraptured with kissing balls, Lord Hawke."

"No. Not until they become big boys."

She laughed, and he looked up quickly, a return grin rising to his lips. "What of Abby and Mrs. Norris? Can they help?"

"I don't like to ask. They'll be overwhelmed with their own tasks for the fete."

He bandaged the worst of the cuts on her fingers, then reached for her other hand. "I daresay we can find a few girls in the village who'd like to earn some extra guineas making kissing balls."

She glanced up at him, surprised. "That's kind of you, my lord."

"Yes, well, I wouldn't get used to it, Miss Templeton. I'm certain to be back to snarling soon enough."

"I'll consider myself properly forewarned." She flexed her hands, admiring his handiwork. "Your bandages are very tidy. You're quite good at treating wounds."

"Ryan and Etienne are forever scraping themselves bloody. Over time I became handy with the salve, although..." he paused, his smile dimming. "I'm a bit out of practice now."

There was no mistaking the hint of guilt in his voice, and goodness, she was weepy today, because before she knew it, tears threatened again. Impulsively, she reached out and took his hand. "Not so out of practice, my lord."

Perhaps he heard the hitch in her voice, because he looked up, and his gaze caught hers. It roamed over her face, and the expression in those dark green depths...well, she couldn't quite read it, but it made heat flood her cheeks, and all at once she was trembling, and she didn't know why, except that he was closer than he had been a moment before, much closer, his eyes flicking back and forth between her eyes and her lips, and she was meant to do something, wasn't she? Something...but she didn't know what.

Confused, she dropped her gaze, but he wouldn't allow that. He touched two long fingers to her chin and turned her face back up to his. "No, perhaps not so out of practice, after all," he murmured, his voice husky.

She swallowed, her breath suddenly coming more quickly, her skin tingling as every inch of her strained toward him. "My lord?"

He was going to kiss Helena Templeton.

He had no right to do it—no right to touch her at all, but she was so close, her sweet red mouth just a breath away from his and her eyes wide, invitation in those blue-gray depths. So lovely, her eyes, like a winter sky before the morning haze melted away. He wanted to fall into them and stay there forever.

He'd been waiting a lifetime to kiss her, hadn't he?

An entire lifetime...

He clasped her face in his hands and touched the tip of his thumb to the seam of her lips, gently parting them. "Your mouth is so sweet, Helena."

"I...is it?" She let out a shaky laugh, but she made no move to pull away, just looked up at him with eyes gone a deep, sleepy gray.

"Yes. So pretty, love."

Could she read the desire in his eyes? She was naïve, an innocent...

A kiss, then. Only a kiss.

He let his lips hover over hers for one breath, two, giving her a chance to pull away, but she only gazed up at him, her eyes soft.

Just like that, he was lost.

He leaned closer, and brushed the gentlest kiss over her parted lips.

She went still, as if stunned by the kiss, but then she let out a breathy sigh, and her hands drifted over his chest. He stiffened for an instant, certain she was going to push him away, but she only rested them there, her palms flat against his chest, warming him.

"Let me...I need to taste you here." He drew back, groaning when her mouth chased his, and brushed his lips over the soft skin behind her ear, his breath leaving his lungs in a hoarse rasp when he felt her pulse flutter wildly against his tongue.

She stroked her fingers over his jaw, tracing the angles of it, a little sound of pleasure dropping from her lips. "Oh, that feels...it tickles."

She urged his mouth back to hers, her tongue meeting his in a single shy stroke—such an innocent caress, yet her eagerness had him breathless and panting as he searched for more of her silken warmth, a pained groan on his lips.

She made a low, needy sound in her throat and opened her mouth against his, chasing his tongue, coaxing it inside and...

Dear God. She was sucking on his tongue.

Everything dropped away then—the work table, the tangled branches, the white ribbons. There was only *her*, her slender body trembling against his, her mouth warm and eager.

He kissed her and kissed her, his tongue plundering the depths of her mouth, his body aching with a desire he'd thought lost to him forever. "So sweet, Helena. You're so sweet."

She shivered against him, squirming closer with every stroke of his tongue. Her breath tickled his ear, her hands moving restlessly over his chest. Such small, dainty hands, but so warm, her touch the most exquisite heat, searing him.

He slid his hands into her hair, hairpins scattering in the wake of his seeking fingers, the heavy locks tumbling to her shoulders. He cupped her neck, desire overwhelming him at the sensation of her warm skin against his palms. God, he couldn't get enough of her neck, couldn't tear his gaze away from it, couldn't keep his hands off that hint of creamy skin above the high collar of her gown that had so transfixed him at the church this morning.

"I want to kiss you here." No, he wanted to *start* there, and then keep going until he'd tasted every inch of her. "May I, sweetheart?"

"Yes." Her voice was low, breathy, without a hint of hesitation.

His fingertips danced up her spine to the buttons at the neck of her gown, teasing them open so he could stroke that delicate skin, lave it with his tongue. Would it be as soft as it looked, sliding like silk against his lips? He had to find out, had to know...

He dipped his head so he could trail his lips down her neck, sucking and nibbling, then soothing the sting with gentle strokes of the tip of his tongue.

"*Adrian.*" She sank her fingers into his hair, tugging him closer.

"Do you need more, sweetheart?" He stroked his tongue over the pulse point at the base of her neck. "Do you want more, Helena?"

She made a strangled sound, something between a sigh and a gasp, and he swept his fingers over her throat to feel the movement, then leaned closer and brushed his lips over the curve where her neck met her shoulder, and God, it was sweet, her skin softer than anything he'd ever touched, a faint scent of fresh greenery clinging to her, the scent surrounding him, teasing his senses until he was drunk with it, every inch of him aching for her, his reason fleeing in the face of a desire that sent him to his knees.

It was meant to be a kiss only, just one kiss...

But he couldn't make himself let her go. Instead of setting her away from him as he should have done, he wrapped his hands around her slender waist, his fingers curling into the delicious curve of her hips. "Come here, sweetheart, let me..." He urged her to her feet and pressed her back against the table, one hand sliding up her spine and into the open neck of her gown.

"Adrian." She wrapped her arms around his neck and pressed her mouth to the hollow of his throat, sucking a fold of his skin between her teeth and nipping at him.

"Ah." He shuddered, his head swimming with need, and pressed her closer, his body crushed to hers. He could feel the shape of her thighs and her breasts, and God, she felt so good, her soft curves such a perfect fit against him, her belly cradling his aching cock.

"Adrian," she moaned. "Please."

Then he was whispering to her, jumbled words of need and desire, his mouth hot against her ear and his hands on her hips, mere seconds away from forgetting himself entirely and lifting her onto the table, his hand fisted in her skirts, and God knew what might have happened if his elbow hadn't hit the basket, and sent it toppling to the floor, white ribbons spilling from the top of it.

He blinked, dazed, then tore his mouth from hers with a defeated groan. This was madness. She wasn't some London courtesan, but his sons' governess, and an innocent. "This isn't...we can't..." He leaned forward to rest his forehead against hers and tried to catch his breath. "You need to go upstairs now, sweetheart."

For a moment she seemed not to understand, her fingers curling in his shirt as she gazed up at him, her touch stealing every breath he'd struggled for, but as the silent moments ticked by, the haze of her desire dissipated, and he saw the exact instant when she realized where she was, what they'd done.

Her hands dropped away from him. "Oh, dear. Yes, I—I think that would be best."

It took everything in him not to snatch her back into his arms, but he settled for brushing a chaste kiss on her forehead.

Mostly chaste. For now, that is.

This wouldn't be the last time he kissed Helena Templeton. "Goodnight, Helena."

She peeked up at him from under her eyelashes, her cheeks pink. "Goodnight, Lord Hawke."

"Adrian." Touching her again was dangerous, but he caught one of her loose curls and twined it around his finger before releasing her and stepping back, away from those temptingly swollen red lips. "Sweet dreams, sweetheart."

CHAPTER
THIRTEEN

Helena didn't sleep at all that night, but this time it had nothing to do with the kittens. Kittenish antics weren't, as it happened, any match for an earl's kisses when it came to depriving a lady of her rest.

Though perhaps it wasn't earls' kisses in general, but only Adrian's kisses. Yes, *his* kisses were the reason she'd memorized the length, width and direction of every crack in the ceiling directly above her bed.

She'd floated up the stairs last night, her fingers pressed to her swollen lips, Adrian's whispered words in her ears, imagining that the most delicious dreams awaited her. Dreams of his mouth taking hers, his lips softer than any mans' should be, the silky glide of his hair against her fingertips, and the gentle stroke of his hands over her heated skin.

But as night crept toward day it brought reality with it, as surely as it brought the frigid morning air that crept under her coverlet and bit her toes.

She didn't have any business kissing Adrian. Phee needed her, and she would never turn her back on her sister. She was leaving Hawke's Run, leaving them all behind, and that was the end of it.

But Lady Anne wasn't going anywhere. Sweet, affectionate Lady Anne, with her pretty blue eyes and infectious smile. Lady Anne, who was born to be a countess, and who would love Ryan and Etienne almost as much as she herself did.

Instead of kissing Adrian, she should be encouraging him to kiss Lady Anne, even if the thought of his lips roaming over Lady Anne's fair skin did cause a wrench in her chest that left her gasping.

But she was a Templeton sister, and the Templeton sisters were matchmakers. Not that it took a matchmaker to see that there wasn't a lady in England who was a better match for Adrian than Lady Anne. It was a happily-ever-after in the making.

It just wasn't *her* happily-ever-after. She was only getting in the way of what was meant to be. So, for the first time since she'd spied him sneaking into the stables, she didn't hurry to the window seat when the clock chimed the four o'clock hour, but remained flat on her back in her bed, every limb rigid, and waited until she was certain he'd been to see Hecate and then gone again.

Only then did she rise, dress and make her way to the stables. Hecate was rolling about on her warm flannel with the remains of last night's lamb stew in a dish beside her, looking quite pleased with herself. "Spoiled thing." She scratched Hecate under the chin, but otherwise didn't linger, leaving the cat purring contentedly.

She found Mrs. Norris laboring over the fire in the kitchens.

"Oh, good morning, Miss Templeton." Mrs. Norris

turned from her task when the door opened. "You're up early."

"We're both earlier than usual this morning. Here, I'll do that." Helena took the tinderbox from the housekeeper and soon had the fire burning, and had set the kettle on to boil. "I rose early this morning to check on Hecate."

"Ah. How does Miss Hecate do this morning? Any kittens yet?"

"Not yet, no, but it won't be long now. You can't imagine how excited Ryan and Etienne are. They're beside themselves with anticipation."

"It's a good thing you're doing, Miss Templeton, teaching those boys how to be kind to animals. I don't know that they ever would have learned such a thing, if not for you." Mrs. Norris sighed, shaking her head.

"I'm not so certain. Are you aware, Mrs. Norris, that Lord Hawke has risen before daybreak every morning this week to check on Hecate? He even changed the hay in her pen, and brought her a flannel."

Mrs. Norris gaped at her over the edge of her teacup. "Did he, now? Well, I'll be."

"I wouldn't have believed it if I hadn't seen the evidence myself." Helena shook her head. Her heart was crumbling in her chest, yet a smile rose to her lips, all the same. Adrian and Hecate were quite a pair. "He, ah...he doesn't seem to care much for cats."

"Mayhap not, but he does care for his boys, and make no mistake." Mrs. Norris set her teacup in its saucer with a click. "He loves them something fierce, for all that it may seem as though he doesn't."

"I don't question Lord Hawke's devotion to his sons, Mrs. Norris. I confess I did so, at first, but Lord

Hawke is...nothing at all like the man I thought he was." Oh, dear, perhaps that was just a bit too frank. She raised her teacup hastily to her lips to keep any more revealing words from escaping. "Er, where's Abby this morning?"

"I sent her off to scrub the staircase and polish the banisters. We're to have the ladies from the Benevolent Society over today to decorate for the Christmas fete, you know, and I don't want them looking askance at my banisters."

"No, indeed not. I beg your pardon, Mrs. Norris, for all the extra work the fete has caused you. I was the one who suggested we have it here once we discovered Goodall Abbey had flooded."

"Nonsense, Miss Templeton. It's for the Poor Fund, and I don't mind telling you I quite like that we're to have it here, despite the fuss. It reminds me of happier times at Hawke's Run. Lady Hawke did love a party, you know, and she adored Christmas."

There was a portrait of the late Countess of Hawke in the second-floor portrait gallery. Helena had spent hours gazing at it since she'd come to Hawke's Run, fascinated by that arresting face, the laughing blue eyes. Lady Sophie had been a beauty, with dark, lustrous hair, and a mouth so like a rosebud one would imagine she only ever uttered the sweetest words, if it hadn't been for the impudent curve at the corners of her lips. "She looks like the sort of lady who would."

"I don't excuse his lordship's shortcomings, but anyone who'd met Lady Sophie can't help but understand how sharply he feels her loss. I've never seen a man more in love with a woman than Lord Hawke was with Lady Sophie."

Helena hesitated, but it wasn't often she had a chance to speak to Mrs. Norris privately, and she wasn't going to get an opening better than this one. She waited for the kettle to boil, then prepared a tea tray and joined the housekeeper at the table. "What was Lady Hawke like, Mrs. Norris?"

"Oh, she was the prettiest little thing you ever saw, Miss Templeton. She had a sharp tongue about her, though, for all that you wouldn't guess it to look at her, with those big blue eyes of hers. The boys look rather like her, you know. Well, except for their green eyes. Those are pure Lord Hawke, those eyes."

Helena smiled. "Yes, I noticed that about him right away."

Mrs. Norris stirred her tea, but she seemed miles away. "Lord Hawke has always tried to do right by his boys," she said at last. "He didn't leave Hawke's Run for an entire year after Lady Hawke passed, but perhaps he should have done."

"What do you mean?"

"It was dreadfully difficult for him to be here once Lady Hawke was gone, with the boys asking for her every day. By the time his year of mourning was over, he was desperate to get away." Mrs. Norris turned her teacup in the saucer. "It started with a business trip to London, but then...ah, well, grief is a strange thing. I think he wanted to lose himself, and sure enough, he found a way to do it. He's been trying to find his way back ever since, but he hasn't been able to quite see his way clear."

"I—I see." God in heaven, how dreadfully unfair to Adrian she'd been! She hadn't thought it her place to pry into his personal life, but she should have done, because all these months she'd assumed he was another selfish aristocrat, when really, he was just a man with a broken heart. "Thank you for telling me this, Mrs. Norris."

"I expect you've a right to know, being the boys' governess. There's plenty as haven't a kind word to say about Lord Hawke, claiming he's a rake, and such. His lordship hasn't confided in me, mind you, but he never ran off to London to become a rake. He went to escape Hawke's Run."

"But not the boys, surely? I can't imagine he wished to escape them."

"No." Mrs. Norris took a thoughtful sip of her tea as she considered the question. "It's not the boys he's running from, Miss Templeton, it's the memories of what Hawke's Run once was to him. The worst of it is, he can't escape them that way, any more than anyone else can. Anyone who's ever suffered a loss knows that, but Lord Hawke, well...he's struggled to accept what is."

Helena stared down at her hands. Mrs. Norris was right, of course. She'd spent many months raging at her mother for abandoning their family, and many more mourning her father's heartbreaking decline and death. Even now, more than a year later, her fingers had gone tight around the handle of her teacup just thinking about it.

"I don't deny his lordship can be a bit trying at times, but don't you get discouraged, Miss Templeton." Mrs. Norris patted her hand. "You've done those boys a world of good at a time when they desperately needed a friend, and that's something, it is. It matters."

Now was the moment to tell Mrs. Norris the truth, to confess that she'd soon have to leave

Hawke's Run and return to Herefordshire, but Helena's throat was too tight to speak.

"And now we're to have a Christmas party! I don't say it'll be like old times again—one can't go back to the past, Miss Templeton, nor should one wish to—but Lord Hawke's been different since he came home, a bit more like himself. I have hopes he may be able to see his way forward, at last. I'm rather glad Goodall Abbey flooded, if you want the truth."

Goodall Abbey. Helena bit her lip. Did she dare ask? "Lord Hawke seems to be well-acquainted with Lady Goodall and...and Lady Anne." She stumbled a little over the name, and her cheeks flooded with heat. "I gather they've known each other for some time?"

"Oh, yes. Lady Anne has spent a good deal of time at Goodall Abbey over the years. She and Lord Hawke grew up together, and they've always been fond of each other. Lady Goodall and Lord Hawke's mother were great friends, you know. It was their dearest wish that Lady Anne and Lord Hawke would marry one day, but fate has her way in the end, doesn't she?"

"Yes, I suppose she does." But then perhaps fate wasn't quite finished with Adrian and Lady Anne? Perhaps she'd been biding her time, waiting for her moment. There must be a reason why it all fit together so neatly now, mustn't there?

Like a puzzle finally coming together, all its pieces in the proper place.

"Well, I'd best go and find out what Abby's getting up to, and tell her I've got some of the village girls coming today to help her clean. That'll cheer her up." Mrs. Norris chuckled as she got to her feet. "That girl's never happier than when she has someone to order about."

Helena remained in the kitchen, her teacup between her hands, and thought about Ryan, Etienne and Adrian, and heartbreak, and the grief that had nearly torn the three of them apart.

By the time her tea had cooled, she'd made up her mind.

Now it was simply a matter of seeing the thing done.

"I'M AFRAID THIS WON'T DO, MISS TEMPLETON." LADY Codswaddle poked at one of the kissing balls, her lip curled with disdain.

Adrian had been as good as his word and had secured a few girls from the village to help her with the kissing balls, but Helena had still spent the better part of the afternoon in the stillroom with a lapful of greenery and ribbons, struggling over the last of them. The bandages that Adrian had so carefully wrapped around her fingers were in shreds, her arms were aching, and she'd nearly gone cross-eyed from tying ribbons.

In short, she'd had quite enough of Lady Codswaddle's endless complaints, and she was perhaps far less cordial than she might have been when she asked, "What's the matter *this* time?"

"Why, there aren't enough of them, of course. I imagined six dozen would do, but we must have one for each of the sconces. They'll look very well beside the pier glasses."

There were two sconces fixed into each of the panels that lined the ballroom, each pair with a pier glass between them, and at least...Helena did a rough count.

A dozen panels. To accommodate Lady Codswaddle's demands, she'd need another *two* dozen kissing balls, not a dozen.

"These are rather small, aren't they?" Lady Codswaddle took up a kissing ball and held it up to one of the sconces. "Well, you see for yourself what I mean, Miss Templeton."

Helena *didn't* see, but before she could unclench her teeth and say so Adrian, who'd been helping Lady Anne drape greenery around the mantelpiece descended on them, his lips tight. "Is there a problem, Lady Codswaddle?"

"Lord Hawke, thank goodness you're here. I'm afraid we do have rather a problem, yes. There are simply not enough kissing balls, you see. I'm of the mind we need another dozen, at least, but Miss Templeton doesn't appear to agree with me."

"Neither do I, madam." Adrian waved a hand around the ballroom. "We're overrun with kissing balls as it is. I can't stir a step without one of them slapping me in the forehead, for God's sake."

Lady Codswaddle drew herself up with a sniff. "As the head of the decorations committee, my lord, I must insist—"

"No more kissing balls, Lady Codswaddle. We're already choking on them as it is."

Lady Codswaddle sucked in an outraged breath, but Helena interrupted her before she could unleash another tirade. She was simply too dispirited to argue over something as silly as kissing balls. The fete would be over after tomorrow night, and none of this would matter anymore. "It's alright, my lord. I don't mind making another dozen." She *did* mind, and she suspected Adrian knew it, but—

Lord Hawke, that is. He was *Lord Hawke*, not Adrian, for pity's sake.

Surely that wasn't so difficult to remember? Just because he'd kissed her with his impossibly soft lips, and stroked his fingers up her spine and loosened the buttons of her gown and nuzzled her neck and whispered her name...

Wait, what point had she been making?

Oh, yes. Nothing had changed between them. He was still the earl and she was still his sons' governess, at least for another few days, and governesses didn't call their employers by their Christian names. "Abby and I can assemble them this evening, but I'll have to climb the alder tree to get more mistletoe. We've run out."

"Climb the alder tree! Are you mad?"

Adrian—dash it, Lord Hawke—was glaring at her. "It's no bother—"

"You're not going up that tree, Hel...that is, Miss Templeton. It'll be dark soon, and it looks as if it's going to snow."

Lady Codswaddle sniffed. "I confess I don't see what all the fuss is, my lord. Miss Templeton looks spry enough. I'm certain she can scamper right up there and be back down again in a trice. It can't be terribly difficult, after all."

Adrian turned on Lady Codswaddle, his hands clenched as if it was taking all his restraint not to throttle her. "If it's so simple, then why don't you go up yourself?"

"Me? Oh no, Lord Hawke. I'm afraid that's impossible. I must be off now. I don't like to ride in my carriage in the snow. It's not safe, you know. Goodbye!" Lady Codswaddle waved her fingertips at Lady Anne, and then swept out in a bustle of silk skirts.

"Helena," Adrian began, his voice low. "This is madness. You're not going up that tree."

She avoided his gaze. "I've done it dozens of times, my lord. I'll be perfectly safe."

"Safe! Last time you climbed up there I had to come up and get you!"

"I'll take better care with my hair this time."

"Helena." He reached for her, but something in her expression must have given him pause, because he dropped his hand without touching her. "I'll go up myself, if I have to, but you're not climbing that bloody tree. I forbid it."

Forbid it? Oh, dear. That hadn't been the right thing to say at all. "Very well, my lord. Since you forbid it, I won't climb the alder tree."

His eyes narrowed suspiciously. "That's it? No further arguments?"

"Of course not, my lord." Why should she argue over the alder tree when one of the silver maples lining the drive had plenty of mistletoe?

She turned to go, but he caught her wrist before she could take a step, and lowered his voice to a whisper. "Wait, Helena. Don't think I haven't noticed you've been avoiding me all day, but you can't hide from me forever. As enormous as this castle is, I *will* find you."

His hot green eyes held hers, and dear God, she wanted nothing more than to slide her arms around his neck and sink into him, but just as she was in danger of doing just that, she caught sight of Lady Anne over his shoulder, tying long lengths of wide velvet ribbon into elegant bows, a pretty flush coloring her cheeks.

"Your guest is waiting for you, my lord."

"Listen to me, Helena. I want—"

He didn't get any further, because she tugged her wrist from his grasp and fled the ballroom.

But she had little enough reason to congratulate herself for her escape. She spent another sleepless night tossing in her bed, wondering with everything inside her how Adrian would have finished that sentence, if only she could have given him the chance.

FOURTEEN

T he ballroom was drowning in kissing balls.

Everywhere Adrian looked—the mantelpiece, the wall sconces, the brightly lit chandeliers above his head, even the backs of the gilt chairs arranged around the outskirts of the ballroom —were smothered in kissing balls. If there was a flat surface or an unadorned protrusion to be found, Lady Codswaddle had draped or dangled a kissing ball atop it.

Or rather Helena had, at her ladyship's insistence.

Christmas had come to Hawke's Run with a vengeance, and cast up its accounts all over his ballroom.

Between the kissing balls, Lady Codswaddle's imperious demands, and Cook's hysteria over the supper menu, he could hardly blame Helena if she was heartily sick of the Christmas fete, and spent the entire evening hiding in her bedchamber.

He could blame her for other things, though.

It had been three days since he'd kissed her in the stillroom—three days that had spun into an eternity because since then, he'd scarcely spoken two dozen words to Helena. Every time he got within touching distance of her, she either fled in the other direction, or somehow maneuvered it so he was obliged to shift his attention to Lady Anne.

It didn't make any bloody *sense*.

It had been, of course, the height of impropriety for him to have kissed her at all. A proper gentleman didn't kiss his sons' governess, particularly not a proper gentleman who wasn't proper at all, but rather a scandalous rake.

Helena was an *innocent*, for God's sake. Even if she did agree to listen to him, what could he say? He hadn't any excuse for losing control as he'd done. None of the thousand words that rushed to his lips whenever he saw her face felt like enough.

Yet as tangled as things with Helena had become, he couldn't make himself regret kissing her. No man could *ever* regret a kiss like that one—a kiss that seized his body and soul, a kiss that left him so shaken it was as if Helena had reached directly into his chest and wrapped her warm, gentle fingers around his beating heart.

He'd only ever experienced one kiss like it before, and that was the first time he'd kissed Sophie. He'd recognized that kiss as the revelation it was then, and he recognized it again now.

For reasons he couldn't fathom, fate had gifted him with a miraculous second chance at another great love, and he had no intention of squandering it. Helena might duck and dodge and evade him as much as she liked, but he'd never give up chasing her until he made her his.

He'd chase her to the ends of the earth if he had to, and since they'd shared that dizzying kiss, it was beginning to look as if he would have to do just that. Over the past few days, he'd spent so much time skirting around corners and wandering empty corridors in search of her, he'd begun to feel like a dull-witted cat doomed to chase a very beautiful, very clever mouse though his very large castle for all eternity.

She was driving him mad—

"Oh, Lord Hawke, here you are." Lady Goodall swept up to him, her face lighting up as she took in the ballroom. "Goodness, how pretty everything looks lit up with candlelight! The decorations committee outdid themselves, did they not, my lord?"

"Indeed, my lady." He bowed over Lady Goodall's hand, then turned to Lady Anne with a smile. She was wearing a gown of cream-colored silk tonight, and had little sprigs of holly scattered through her fair hair. "You see the fruits of all your labors tonight, Lady Anne. Are you pleased with it?"

"My, yes! It's perfectly lovely, my lord." Lady Anne glanced around, and her bright smile turned mischievous. "Though I can't help but notice there are quite a surfeit of kissing balls."

Lady Goodall laughed. "Hush, Anne, you naughty thing. Go and fetch my wrap from the carriage for me, won't you, dear? I'm a trifle chilled."

"Yes, aunt." Lady Anne paused at the window on her way to the door, and her eyes went wide. "My goodness, it looks as if there are a dozen carriages waiting in the drive! I daresay our Christmas fete is going to be a crush."

"You'd best hurry then, Anne," Lady Goodall said, "Or you'll be caught in the crush and it will take ages for you to make your way back to the ballroom."

"Yes, aunt. I'm going."

Lady Goodall waited until Lady Anne was gone, then she drew Adrian aside. "If I might have a quick word, Lord Hawke?"

"Of course, my lady. How can I help?"

"I thought it would be lovely if you opened the ball by dancing the first dance with Anne. Is that agreeable to you, my lord?"

"Dance with Lady Anne?" He hadn't given any thought at all to dancing, but he'd have to, wouldn't he?

"Anne is the chair of the Ladies' Benevolent Society, as you know, my lord, and as you are the evening's host it only seems proper that you dance the first dance together, but if you have some other young lady in mind—"

"No, no. I'd be delighted to open the ball with Lady Anne." It wasn't as if he could refuse, and he had no objection to Lady Anne. They were friends, after all, and it wasn't as if he could have the lady he truly wanted. Helena was certain to keep well away from the ballroom tonight.

"Lovely!" Lady Goodall beamed at him. "Here comes Anne now. I daresay she'll be delighted to dance with you, my lord."

Lady Anne accepted his invitation to dance with her usual grace, then she and Lady Goodall made their way into the ballroom while he remained where he was to see to his guests as they arrived.

It was a crush, just as Lady Anne had predicted. The Ladies' Benevolent Society fete was always well attended—one couldn't be seen to be slighting the Poor Fund, after all—but the throng that made their way up the stairs and into Hawke's Run's ballroom put every previous year's fete to shame. Some of the guests had even come from as far away as Chipping Norton, but judging by the way some of them gawked at him and whispered behind their hands, it wasn't the generous Christmas spirit that had lured them here.

No, they'd come to get a glimpse at one of London's most notorious rakes for themselves.

Whatever the reason for the crush, the guests were still arriving by the time the grandfather clock chimed the ten o'clock hour, so he made his way over to Lady Anne, and bowed over her hand. She offered him a pretty curtsy in return, and he led her to the dance floor to the opening strains of a minuet.

And so, the St. Mary's Ladies Benevolent Society Christmas Fete had begun.

Despite the cold and the threat of snow, guests continued to stream into the ballroom over the next hour. It was so crowded that by the end of the first two dances two young ladies had swooned from the heat, and they were obliged to open a window. The entire party was in high spirits, and encouraged in their merriment by generous servings of negus and mulled wine. Even Lady Codswaddle pronounced the evening to be 'perfectly agreeable' and deemed the guests to be 'the very height of elegance.'

Adrian smiled and laughed and danced, but there was one face missing amongst all the pretty faces surrounding him, a young lady with golden-brown curls and blue-gray eyes.

The ballroom felt empty without her.

"WHY DIDN'T YOU GO TO THE BALL, MISS TEMPLETON?" Ryan asked, tugging on Helena's hand. "Don't you like to dance?"

Helena *did* like to dance, but there'd never been any question of her doing so tonight. Servants didn't attend their employer's Christmas fetes.

Ninety-four kissing balls notwithstanding.

It had never bothered her before, being a servant. Governess was a perfectly respectable occupation for an educated lady of slender means, yet now, peering down on the ballroom below from behind a screen on one of the balconies, her stomach was twisting with bitterness, jealousy and regret.

Goodness, when did Christmas become such a miserable holiday?

She would have done well to keep far away from the ballroom tonight, but the boys were excited about the fete, and it didn't seem fair to deny them a peek at the festivities. So, she'd given them each a piece of Cook's gingerbread and taken them to the balcony, once she'd secured their promise to go to bed without a fuss afterwards.

"Do you even know *how* to dance, Miss Templeton?" Etienne gave her a doubtful look.

"I do, indeed, but I'm here with you and Ryan. I can hardly be in two places at once, can I?"

"I think you should dance, if you like it, Miss Templeton. All the other ladies are dancing." Ryan peered down at the whirl of couples below them, his green eyes alight with interest. "Papa can dance."

She stifled a sigh. He could, indeed. It was impossible not to watch him, as tall and graceful as he was, and so handsome in his formal evening clothes. More than one young lady had cast an admiring glance at him as he'd led Lady Anne to the floor for the first dance, and he'd danced every set since then, just as a proper host should do.

"But maybe Miss Templeton doesn't have a ball dress." Etienne nibbled at his gingerbread. "I think it's a rule that a lady has to have a ball dress to go to a ball. Is that right, Miss Templeton?"

"Not a rule, perhaps, but yes, a lady wouldn't wish to appear at a ball without the proper attire."

"Jewels, too." Ryan leaned so far over the balcony railing Helena was obliged to snatch him by the collar and pull him back. "A lady has to have lots of jewels. Isn't that right, Miss Templeton?"

"I suppose so, yes." Certainly, most of the ladies here tonight were wearing them. Lady Codswaddle was so smothered in emeralds she looked like a kissing ball herself. It was rather disconcerting, really.

"Lady Anne is wearing jewels," Etienne observed. "Sparkly ones, in her ears."

"Those are diamonds, and she has a string of pearls around her neck." She drew in a breath, and forced the next words from her lips. "She, ah...she looks very pretty, doesn't she?"

Dear God, that had taken an effort, and it shouldn't have. Indeed, she was ashamed of herself for the jealousy burning a hole in her chest. Lady Anne *did* look pretty, and if Lord Hawke thought so too, as he certainly appeared to do, well...that was what she wanted, wasn't it?

She'd be gone from Hawke's Run soon enough. All that mattered was that Lord Hawke remained here with Ryan and Etienne once she was gone.

Ryan, Etienne and...and Lady Anne.

"She's not as pretty as you are, Miss Templeton,"

Etienne announced, with all the sweet loyalty of a six-year-old boy.

"Her gown is white," Ryan added in a disapproving tone. "I don't like white gowns. The bright colors are prettier. I like Lady Codswaddle's gown. It's pink."

"No, it isn't! It's brown!" Etienne inspected what was left of his slice of gingerbread, then stuffed the last bite into his mouth. "Brown isn't a pretty color."

No, and even less so when paired with emeralds, for pity's sake. "That color is called puce, and it's a combination of brown, pink and purple."

"Well, I don't like it," Etienne said. "And I don't like Lady Codswaddle."

"Neither do I," Ryan agreed. "She's always scolding."

"Papa doesn't like her, either. I heard him call her a harridan."

"Etienne!" Helena snorted back a laugh. "That is *not* a nice thing to say. I beg you will never repeat that in Lady Codswaddle's hearing. Or in anyone else's hearing, come to that."

"Papa likes Lady Anne, though." Ryan devoured the remainder of his own slice of gingerbread with such gusto crumbs scattered everywhere.

That chased the smile from her face quickly enough. "Does he? How, ah...how do you know that, Ryan?"

"I saw him kiss her," Ryan said around his mouthful of gingerbread.

"Kiss her?" Helena repeated faintly. "You saw your father *kiss* Lady Anne?"

"Mmmhmm." Ryan swallowed the last of his gingerbread and wiped his hands on his nightshirt.

"No, he didn't!" Etienne let out a little shriek of laughter, the idea of his papa kissing a lady being too much for his six-year-old sensibilities.

"Did too," Ryan said stoutly. "Last night, in the ballroom."

Adrian—that is, Lord Hawke—and Lady Anne had been *kissing* in the ballroom?

That was...well, it was...perfectly splendid, of course! Just what she'd hoped would happen. Why, her stomach was absolutely rolling with...happiness. Rolling and turning with it, especially when Lord Hawke once again took Lady Anne's hand, and led her out to the dance floor.

It was their second dance of the evening, though who was counting?

Not *her*, that was certain.

Though two dances in one evening...that was sure to give rise to speculation amongst the other guests. No doubt they were all even now whispering about how well Lord Hawke and Lady Anne looked together, how wonderfully they suited each other.

Because they did. It was all very...wonderful.

Given the way Lord Hawke was smiling down at Lady Anne, it looked as if it might well be *three* dances before the end of the ball. As for Lady Anne, she was stepping gracefully through the figures of a quadrille, her lovely cream-colored silk skirts swirling around her ankles, and gazing up at Adrian as if she'd like nothing more than to find a kissing ball and put it to good use.

Which wouldn't be terribly difficult, given there were ninety-four of the blasted things. "Come along, boys, it's getting late. It's past time for you both to go to bed."

"No! Can't we watch for a little while longer, Miss Templeton?"

They hung onto her hands like two clinging limpets, their eyes wide and pleading. Usually, she had a dreadful time resisting those big green eyes, but this time, she couldn't bear to stay where she was for another minute. "You recall, do you not, boys, that we had an agreement? I permitted you each a bit of gingerbread and a peek at the party, and in return, you're meant to go to bed without a fuss. It's not gentlemanly to break your word."

Ryan exchanged a guilty glance with his brother, and let out a defeated sigh. "Yes, Miss Templeton."

They didn't object again as she led from the balcony down the corridor, and soon enough she had them tucked into the beds, their eyes drooping. "There we are. Sweet dreams, my little gentlemen."

Ryan gave a great yawn. "Will you go and see Hecate before you go to bed, Miss Templeton? I think she may be lonely."

She smoothed his dark hair back from his forehead. "I will, indeed. Now, go to sleep, boys, and when you wake tomorrow morning, it will be Christmas Day."

But as she closed the boys' bedchamber door behind her and made her way through the darkened corridor and down the back staircase—taking care to give the ballroom a wide berth—it didn't feel much like Christmas to her.

It felt like something was slipping through her fingers, and no matter how she clung to it, how she clawed and scratched and struggled to hold onto it, in the end she would have to let it go, and a piece of her heart along with it.

CHAPTER
FIFTEEN

"Helena Eloisa Templeton, you will stop this *instant*!"

Helena's hand was on the knob of the stable door, and she was one twitch of her fingers away from turning it and escaping into the stables where there wouldn't be a single, cursed kissing ball, but at the sound of the familiar voice, she froze.

Eloisa? Dear God, Eloisa...

Not a single person in all of Oxfordshire knew her middle name was Eloisa, except for—

"Not another step. I'm warning you, Helena."

No. It couldn't be!

Except there were only two people in the world who could make her halt in her tracks with a single command. One was Euphemia, but only when she was in a temper. No one ever dared challenge Phee when she was in a temper.

The other was Juliet. No one ever dared challenge Juliet, *ever*.

Slowly she turned around, and there stood her sister in the most mouthwatering rose silk gown Helena had ever seen, her dark hair piled in artful curls atop her head, rubies glittering at her throat and in her ears.

She blinked, then blinked again, but all the blinking in the world wasn't going to change that fact that Juliet had somehow magically appeared in the stable yard at Hawke's Run, and was standing there with her arms crossed over her chest looking very displeased, indeed. "Juliet, for pity's sake, what in the world are you doing—"

"Why didn't you tell me you were in love with Lord Hawke?"

Helena's mouth dropped open. "*What*?"

"Why," Juliet repeated in the calm, measured tone that warned she was very angry, indeed. "Didn't you tell me you were in love with Lord Hawke?"

"I don't—"

"No." Juliet held up her hand. "Don't even bother trying to tell me you're not in love with him, because I know better. Now, let's try this again, shall we? Why, Helena, did you sit across from me in the drawing room at Steeple Cross—for *hours* on end, mind you— without confessing a single word about the fact that you've fallen madly in love with Lord Hawke?"

Madly? More like hopelessly. "What are you even *doing* here?" Yes, that was very good. Perhaps she could stall Juliet while she thought up a plausible lie in response to her sister's other question.

Juliet huffed. "Did you not notice, Helena, that there's a Christmas fete in progress in the ballroom right now?"

"Of course, I noticed it! Who do you suppose made all those blasted kissing balls? Look at my hands!" Helena held up her bandaged fingers.

"Ninety-four kissing balls, Juliet. *Ninety-four*. Do you realize how long it takes to make ninety-four kissing balls? I've spent the last five days dreaming about kissing balls!"

Oh, dear. She was beginning to sound a trifle unhinged.

But Juliet merely raised an eyebrow at this outburst. "Miles and I came for the fete, of course. You didn't imagine I was going to pass up the chance to see Lord Hawke for myself, did you?"

"I didn't imagine anything at all!" But she should have. Steeple Cross was only an hour's carriage ride from Hawke's Run, and hence it was part of the same neighborhood. She should have known her sister and Lord Cross would appear tonight.

"Quite an oversight on your part, I should say, but perhaps you were distracted on account of your being in love with Lord Hawke. Love tends to sweep all before it, doesn't it?" Juliet brushed past Helena, entered the stables and plopped herself down on top of a hay bale. "Sit, Helena." She nodded at the bale beside hers.

"I'm not a hunting dog," Helena muttered crossly, but a childhood spent doing as her elder sisters bid her made her sit down beside Juliet, hay tickling her backside. "You'll ruin your gown, you know."

Juliet didn't reply, but regarded her in silence just long enough to make Helena squirm before at last letting out a long sigh. "I expected to find you in the ballroom this evening, Helena."

"I don't know why you should have. I'm the *governess*, Juliet, not the countess. Governesses don't attend balls."

"I did not expect," Juliet went on, ignoring Helena's comment, "to find you hiding behind a screen on the balcony with Ryan and Etienne, gazing down at Lord Hawke and looking as if you were about to burst into tears."

"You *saw* us?" But she'd taken such care to make certain they were out of sight! Dear God, had Lord Hawke seen them, as well?

"I did, yes, but I don't think anyone else did. I only spotted you because I knew to look there. You remember the balls at Hambleden Manor, don't you?"

"I do, yes." Whenever their parents used to have balls at home, she, Juliet and Phee would hide on the balcony and spy on the proceedings, marveling at the pretty silk gowns and the handsome gentlemen. Of course, that had been before their mother's scandal, back when they'd still had friends. "And I *wasn't* about to burst into tears."

Juliet sat quietly, toying with the heavy stones around her neck. When she did speak, her voice was far gentler than it had been before. "You act as if you think you can fool me, Helena. Do you suppose I can't tell when your heart is breaking? I'm your sister, dearest. I only had to glance at you to see it. Why didn't you tell me?"

Helena slumped atop her hay bale, all her righteous anger draining from her in an instant, leaving her shaking. There was no hiding anything from Juliet, or any of her sisters. There never had been. "I didn't tell you because it doesn't matter, Juliet. Lord Hawke is...well, he's Lord Hawke, isn't he? He's an earl, and I'm a governess, not to mention one of the scandalous Templeton sisters."

"My goodness, Helena, with two sisters so recently married to earls, I would think you'd understand by now that such things as titles and fortunes and scandals are no match for love."

"I might be a royal heiress with a spotless reputation, Juliet, and it wouldn't make any difference. Have you forgotten I'm leaving Hawke's Run? One of us has to return to Hambleden Manor, for Phee's sake."

"I asked you to return to Herefordshire *before* I knew you were in love with Lord Hawke, Helena. It changes everything. Surely, you must see that? We'll think of something else, some other way to—"

"There isn't another way. We've already been over this, and in any case, you forget one thing, Juliet." Tears threatened, but she held them back and met her sister's eyes. "I may be in love with Lord Hawke, but *he's* not in love with *me*."

"That remains to be seen. He's not in love with Lady Anne, if that's what you're thinking. Anyone can see they're friends only, nothing more."

Not anyone. Helena couldn't see it. What she saw was two people whose mutual fondness for each other was a kiss away from blossoming into love. "I hope you're wrong. Ryan and Etienne need a mother, and Adrian—Lord Hawke—is far more likely to choose Hawke's Run over London if he marries Lady Anne."

Juliet's gaze sharpened. "Ah, now I see this for what it is. You're matchmaking Lord Hawke and Lady Anne!"

"What if I am? You needn't sound so scandalized about it. You dabbled in matchmaking yourself, if you recall."

"Oh, I recall it. If *you* recall, I was meant to go to

London and marry Lord Melrose, only he took one look at Emmeline and fell madly in love with her, and I fell madly in love with Miles, the very last man in England any of us would have considered a proper match for me." Juliet reached between them and took Helena's hand. "Love can't be managed, dearest. It has its own way in the end."

Perhaps it did, but so did fate, and by the way Adrian and Lady Anne had gazed at each other tonight, it seemed fate had already made up her mind.

Gently, Helena drew her hand from Juliet's and rose from her hay bale. "There's nothing to be done, Juliet. Now, if you'll pardon me, I've a pregnant cat to see to before I take myself off to bed."

She didn't wait for Juliet's answer, but one came anyway, after Juliet had left the stables and closed the door behind her. "Nothing to be done, indeed. Very well, Helena, you stubborn thing. I'll just have to see to this myself, won't I?"

A THOUSAND YEARS HAD PASSED SINCE THIS BALL BEGAN, one moment crawling after the next, and eternity unfolding only to reveal another eternity looming behind it.

It was rather like he'd always imagined hell to be. God knew it was hot enough in here to be mistaken for hell, and surely there was no punishment more severe than endless quadrilles?

The supper had been served rather late—the prawns were exquisite, so he'd taken a few for Hecate

—but none of the guests seemed at all inclined to go home to their beds. Some of the more sedate among the company had adjourned to the card room, while the younger people had all rushed back to the ballroom for more dancing and flirting.

Did all balls drag on as interminably as this one? Why wouldn't everyone just go home, for God's sake?

But he seemed to be the only person in the ballroom who wished the festivities to be over. He'd hardly seen Ryan and Etienne at all during the past few days of furious fete preparations, and wanted nothing more at the moment than to see their flushed, sleeping faces.

And then there was Helena.

He'd embarked on this evening wishing for her, had spent every moment since the first dance thinking of her, and it seemed he was to end the evening just as he'd begun it—pining for her like a besotted schoolboy. The idea of going to his bed tonight without seeing her was unbearable, but unless he intended to storm her bedchamber, there wasn't much...

He could storm her bedchamber, couldn't he? Or perhaps not *storm* it, but at least knock, and if she *did* come to the door in her nightdress, well, so be it. He'd bid her goodnight—a chaste goodnight, that is, and she—

"All right there, Hawke? You look a bit flushed."

"I'm very well, indeed, er..." Adrian squinted at the dark-haired man who'd approached him. He looked familiar, but he couldn't quite place—

"Miles Winthrop, Lord Cross. Good God, Hawke, has it been so long you no longer recognize me?"

"Cross?" Adrian stared at the man, incredulous.

He'd seen Cross a time or two at the beginning of the season, so it hadn't been long at all, but Cross looked like an entirely different man tonight. He'd always been a brusque sort of fellow, rather dark and cynical, but now he wore a wide smile that took at least a dozen years off his face. "Cross, by God. How do you do? You look very well."

"I suppose I must, given that shocked look on your face. May I present Lady Cross?" Cross gestured proudly to the tall, slender lady on his arm. "My wife, the Countess of Cross. This is Lord Hawke, Juliet."

"Lady Cross. It's a pleasure to meet you." Lady Cross was a stunning, dark-haired creature, and strangely familiar, somehow, though he couldn't quite put his finger on—

"Lord Hawke, at last," Lady Cross said as Adrian bowed over her hand. "I've heard a great deal about *you*."

"Everyone here has heard a great deal about me, I'm afraid." Adrian gave her a wry smile. "I don't believe any of the St. Mary's Ladies' Benevolent Society fetes have ever attracted *quite* so many guests in the past. It looks as if all of Oxfordshire is here, and all of them gawking shamelessly at me."

Lady Cross laughed. "Indeed, but shame on you, my lord, for implying I listen to gossip. Having been the subject of it often enough myself, I assure you that I don't. No, I know of you from my sister, of course."

"Your sister?" Who the devil was her sister?

He must not have hidden his bafflement as well as he hoped, because Lady Cross's brow furrowed. "Why yes, of course. Your governess, Lord Hawke? Helena Templeton is my sister."

"Helena!" My God, he *must* have misheard her, mustn't he?

Except...a dozen small hints and offhand comments started to come back to him then. Cross's recent marriage, and Helena's weekly visits to Steeple Cross...

God above, how could he have been so dense? Helena's sister wasn't the housekeeper or Lady Cross's lady's maid, she was the Countess of Cross herself! "I, er...forgive me, my lady, I wasn't aware—"

"Oh, dear. I see Helena hasn't been quite as forthcoming as she should have been. I daresay you thought I was the housekeeper, or some such thing, didn't you?"

"The housekeeper!" Lord Cross laughed. "No, indeed. You'd make a perfectly wretched housekeeper, Juliet. You're far too accustomed to having everything your own way."

"Nonsense, my lord. I'm the most accommodating person imaginable."

Lord Cross snorted, and his wife tapped his arm smartly with her fan, smiling up at him. "Hush, you awful man."

Adrian watched them tease each other, amused and mystified at once. Despite their sparring, anyone could see they were utterly besotted with each other. Lord Cross had, by all appearances, found himself the perfect lady.

"I do beg your pardon for taking you so off guard, my lord. I'm afraid Helena can be quite reticent when she wishes to be." Lady Cross hesitated. "I daresay you've heard of the Templeton sisters, Lord Hawke?"

The Templeton sisters...

Juliet Templeton! That was the name that had

been eluding him since that day he'd fished Helena out of the tree and she'd told him her name. There was another sister too, wasn't there? Emily, or...no, it was Emmeline. Emmeline Templeton. Yes, he'd heard *that* name before, and hadn't Lady Cross just made a comment about being the object of *ton* gossip?

"My God, I can't believe I didn't realize it sooner. You're the matchmaking sisters!" That was why Lady Cross looked so familiar to him! She resembled her sister Helena, though Lady Cross had dark blue eyes, rather than Helena's blue-gray.

"Oh, dear." Lady Cross turned to her husband. "He's found us out."

He had, indeed, though God knew it had taken him bloody long enough to put it together, given everyone in London was gossiping about the Templeton sisters.

Emmeline Templeton had recently married the Earl of Melrose, the most sought-after gentleman of the *ton*. Lady Pamela had bored him to tears one evening going on about how Lord Melrose had thrown over Lady Christine Dingley for Emmeline Templeton, because Miss Templeton had beguiled him with some kind of magical perfume, or something equally ridiculous.

He only ever listened to Lady Pamela with half an ear, if that.

But good Lord, the Templeton sisters were even more notorious than *he* was. There'd been something about the mother, too, some scandal a few years ago, well before the matchmaking scandal this season, but it was the loss of two of London's most eligible earls to the Templeton sisters that had the *ton* up in arms.

"Judging by your expression, Lord Hawke, may I

assume Helena has not been forthcoming about our family, either?"

"Er, no. That is, she didn't hide it, but..." She hadn't divulged it, either.

Lady Cross laid a hand on his arm. "I beg you won't hold it against her, Lord Hawke. There's been so much gossip, you see, and all of it dreadful, and Helena is a bit more sensitive than—"

"Please, Lady Cross. You needn't worry. I would never...I think the world of Helena. I'm in lo...that is, nothing could ever make me think badly of her," he finished lamely, his face heating.

"I understand perfectly, Lord Hawke." Lady Cross bit her lip. "Forgive me, my lord, but has Helena mentioned to you that she'll soon be obliged to leave Hawke's Run?"

He stared at her. "Leave Hawke's Run?"

"I'm afraid so, yes."

Helena was *leaving* Hawke's Run? Leaving *him*? "When?"

Lady Cross and her husband exchanged uncertain glances. "As soon as the Christmas holidays are over. My elder sister needs her in Herefordshire, and—"

"Forgive me, Lady Cross, and Lord Cross. I must..." He didn't stay to finish the sentence, but turned on his heel.

"She's in the stable, my lord!" Lady Cross called after him.

Adrian strode from the ballroom, ignoring the guests who tried to get his attention.

Did Helena truly believe she could just walk out the door without a single word of explanation, and leave him and his sons heartbroken? Did she truly think he was going to let that happen? Maddening, impossible woman!

He'd made a mess of this, and it was time to put it right once and for all.

Helena wasn't going anywhere.

CHAPTER
SIXTEEN

Another thousand years passed as Adrian raced from the ballroom to the corridor, then down the stairs and through the kitchens to the stables. By the time he pushed the stable door open and stormed inside, his lungs were heaving and his heart was throbbing with hope, fear, anger, tenderness, and thwarted desire.

Because love was all of things at once and more, all snarled tightly together inside him, just waiting for the one person who could tear it apart and launch it springing like a wild thing from his chest.

"Helena!"

In that moment of madness, nothing could keep him from flying to her, dropping to his knees and begging her not to leave him.

Nothing, that is, but what he found.

Helene was hunched over the side of Hecate's pen, but she whirled around when the stable door slammed open, and he stopped in his tracks, his heart plummeting as if it had turned to stone in his chest. Her face was red and blotchy, and she was struggling for breath, her eyes were streaming with tears.

"Helena? Dear God, what is it? What's the matter?"

"It's Hecate! The kittens are...oh, there are so many of them, Adrian! Eight at last count, and..." She went on, but between her hiccups and gasps and sobs he couldn't make sense of what she was saying.

"Helena, listen to me. It's alright, sweetheart." He dropped down into the hay beside her and stroked soothing circles over her back. "Take a deep breath. Yes, that's it. Now, tell me again what's happening."

"I—I thought she'd had all her kittens and was resting, but then she started trying to push again, but she's been pushing for a long time without a kitten coming, and now she's gone very still." She turned big, watery blue gray eyes on him. "There's a kitten lodged in the birth canal, but she's too exhausted to push anymore."

He glanced into the pen. Eight damp puffs of ginger fur with tiny pink paws were crawling on top of each other in the hay, and beside them was Hecate, lying on her side, her eyes closed and her rib cage jerking with quick, panting breaths. "How long has she been like this?"

"An hour? Perhaps longer. I thought of coming to fetch you, but I didn't like to leave her, and I didn't want to drag you away from the ball—"

"The ball doesn't matter, Helena. Don't you understand? Nothing matters to me but you and Ryan and Etienne, and at the moment, Hecate." His boys were *not* going to wake up on Christmas morning to find their beloved pet had died.

It simply wasn't going to happen.

"Right, then." He tore off his evening jacket and handed it to her. "Here, tuck this around the kittens," he said, silently bidding goodbye to another Weston coat. But it was cold, and Hecate was in no state to care for her kittens yet.

He hopped over the side of the pen, knelt in the hay near Hecate's back end, and lifted her tail. "I beg your pardon, Hecate, but I assure you this is as uncomfortable for me as it is for you."

Helena tucked the coat around the squirming kittens nestled in the hay then leaned closer, her fingers clutching the edge of the pen. "Can you see anything?"

"Yes. A leg, and the back end of a, er..." Well, there was really no other way to put it. "A slimy creature I can only assume is a kitten. I don't know much about kitten births, but I suspect I shouldn't be seeing its leg."

"No. It's coming out backwards. I've read a bit about this. Hecate won't be able to push it out on her own." Helena's steady gaze met his, her early distress giving way to determination. "There is a way for us to help her, but it's a bit tricky."

"Tricky or not, I don't see that we have much choice."

She tried to peek around him. "I can't see much. Your shoulders are in my way."

"I beg your pardon, but there's nothing to see at present but a leg protruding from Hecate's...that is, from Hecate. Just tell me what to do, and I'll do it."

"Yes, alright. You'll need a steady grip on the kitten's leg and as much of the torso as you can reach, but be gentle. Don't squeeze, but hold firmly."

"That sounds easier than it is. She's a bit slippery, I'm afraid."

She raised an eyebrow at him. "How do you know it's a she?"

He gave her a quick grin. "Who else but a female kitten would cause such a lot of fuss and bother? There, I've got her. Do I just pull her out?"

"No! Don't pull. You're going to ease her out by rocking her gently from side to side, but you have to wait until Hecate pushes again." Helena stroked her hand over Hecate's head. "I know you're tired, poor thing, but we're not quite finished yet. Come now, Hecate, another push, if you please."

Hecate only spoke cat, of course, so there wasn't any chance she understood these instructions, but damned if she didn't do just as Helena bid her, and gave a weak little push. He peeked under her tail. "Another leg has popped out. Well done, Hecate!"

"That's it, Hecate. Good girl!"

"Surely, the legs are the worst bit? It should be easy enough from here, yes?"

"Er, no, my lord. You've forgotten that the head still has to come out."

The head, yes, and it was rather a bulbous appendage, unfortunately.

"Another push, Hecate," Helena crooned. "Come now, you can do it."

Hecate responded to this plea by giving another push, this one a bit harder than the last. Adrian rocked the kitten from side to side as Helena had instructed, another few inches of the torso emerged. "This kitten looks to be a bit bigger than the others."

"How much of her is out now?"

"There's perhaps a bit more of the torso still to come, then the front paws, shoulders and head."

Good God, there was quite a bit of kitten still to go, and Hecate's breathing was becoming more labored.

"She's exhausted, Adrian. I don't think she's got many pushes left in her. We'll have to have the kitten out with the next one. Did you hear that, Hecate? Just one more push, and then it will be all over, and you can see to your nine beautiful kittens. One more push, Hecate, and that's all."

But this time Hecate didn't respond with a push. Her breathing had become more erratic, and she let her head drop down flat against the stable floor.

"Oh, no, Adrian—"

"Hecate, I've brought you some lovely prawns from the supper buffet tonight. One more push, and they're all yours." It was pure nonsense, of course, to imagine Hecate knew what a prawn was, but he didn't give a damn how foolish it sounded if it got her to give them one last push.

He waited, his fingers wrapped loosely around the kitten's torso, one breath, two...then all at once Hecate let out low, guttural yowl, her body stiffened, and she gave one final, mighty push. "Good girl, Hecate!"

He rocked the small body side to side and watched, fascinated as the remainder of the kitten's torso gave way to the shoulders, then two little curled pink paws, and finally a head, with tiny ears no bigger than his fingernail pressed flat against her head. "I've got her, Helena! She's out!"

"Oh, my goodness, Adrian, I've never seen anything like that before!"

"And I've never *felt* anything like it. Well done, Hecate!"

"You're going to make a wonderful mother, Hecate," Helena murmured, pressing a kiss on the top of Hecate's head.

Now that the largest kitten was out—she was indeed a girl, just as he'd predicted—Hecate perked up, and began nosing at the kittens and licking them vigorously. He watched quietly for a time, then leaned down to wipe his hands on the tails of his coat, as it was ruined anyway. When he felt Helena's eyes on him, he looked up with a smile. "That was not how I imagined this evening would end."

She laughed. "No. It's not quite the Sir Roger De Coverley, is it?"

"No. It was far messier, but now it's over, I can't think of any better way to usher in Christmas Day, can you?"

She opened her mouth, closed it, then opened it again with a shake of her head. "There's something I need to tell you, my lord, and I've put it off for far too long—"

"Oh? Is it that your sister is the Countess of Cross? Or is it that you're one of the infamous matchmaking Templeton sisters that everyone in London is gossiping about?"

She let out a sigh. "I see you've met Juliet."

"Yes." He gazed at her in the dim light of the stables, studying the curve of her cheekbones, the slight upturn of her nose, the adorably stubborn angle of her chin. How had her face become so inexpressibly dear to him in only a few short weeks? "So many secrets, Helena."

"I didn't think you...I never meant to..." She buried her face in her hands. "Oh, dear. I've made a dreadful mess of everything, haven't I?"

"Yes, but no more than I have. It seems neither of us are very good at this." He caught her wrists and lowered her hands from her face. "Don't hide from me, Helena. I don't understand why you didn't simply tell me, sweetheart."

She blinked at the endearment, a blush rushing into her cheeks. "At first I didn't say anything because I thought you'd dismiss me if you knew who I was."

"Dismiss you? Nonsense. Wherever could you have gotten the idea I'd dismiss you?"

That drew a small smile to her lips. "I can't imagine. But I wouldn't have blamed you if you had dismissed me. There aren't many fathers who want a scandalous governess teaching their sons."

"They weren't your scandals, Helena, and even if they had been, it wouldn't have made any difference. Do you think I don't know how much you've done for Ryan and Etienne? There's not a father alive who'd dream of letting you go."

Not a *man* alive, either.

"I still should have told you the truth at once, but I couldn't bear the idea of leaving Ryan and Etienne, so I said nothing, and hoped you wouldn't find out. It was silly of me. Everyone always finds out everything, don't they?"

"In my experience, yes. But there's still something you haven't told me, isn't there, Helena?" He got to his feet, hopped out of the pen and dropped down into the clean hay beside her, because he needed to be closer to her, to be touching her when he told her he...told her—

"There is, yes. I...this is difficult to say." She drew in a deep breath, and met his eyes. "I have to leave Hawke's Run, Adrian. I took the governess position out of financial necessity, but since then two of my sisters have become countesses, and my eldest sister, Euphemia, is lonely with so many of us gone."

"Helena, I—"

"I want you to know that it's not my choice to leave." Her voice broke then, and she dragged an arm across her eyes. "Indeed, I'd much rather stay. I adore the boys, and I'm...very fond of everyone else here, as well."

"Fond?" He eased closer, and caught her chin between his fingers. "Just fond, Helena?"

She blinked up at him, a few tears caught in her dark lashes. "Well, I'm fond of Abby, and Mrs. Norris, yes."

"Hmm." He tipped her chin up, his mouth inching closer to hers. "Anyone else?"

She swallowed. "Hecate, of course, and Hestia and Poseidon."

"Yes?" He brushed his lips over hers, just the lightest caress, then drew back again so he could see into her eyes. "And Artemis, Apollo, Demeter, and Hephaestus? I assume you're fond of all of them, as well?"

"Yes," she whispered.

"I see." He dropped a kiss on her cheek, then let his lips wander over her cheekbone to her temple, the wisps of golden-brown hair there tickling his nose. "Is there anyone else here at Hawke's Run you're fond of, Helena?"

"Not fond, no, but perhaps..." She gasped as he nipped at her earlobe.

"Perhaps?" He closed his hands around her waist and lifted her onto his lap. "Perhaps there's someone here you feel more than fondness for? Perhaps someone you might...love?"

She rested her hands on his chest, but a forlorn sigh slipped from her lips. "Yes, but—"

He covered her hands with his, stroking her fingers. "Might that person be me?"

She pressed her face into his chest to hide it. "Yes, but—"

"No, Helena." He clasped her face in his hands. "Look at me when you tell me you love me."

Her pulse was fluttering in her throat, her beautiful blue gray-eyes searching his. "I *do* love you, Adrian, so very much, but—"

He touched his fingers to her lips to quiet her. "There is nothing else that matters but love, and I love you so much, sweetheart, with everything I have, and everything I am."

"Y—you do?" She peeked up at him from under her eyelashes. "You love me?"

"Yes, you maddening creature, of course, I do. I didn't think I could ever fall in love again, but you took me by surprise, sweetheart. Perhaps it was the mistletoe you threw at me, because I've been mad for you ever since. If you leave Hawke's Run, Helena, you will break my heart into a thousand pieces."

"But...but what about Lady Anne?"

"Ah, Lady Anne. Tell me the truth, Helena. Have you been trying to matchmake me with Lady Anne?"

She shrugged, but a guilty flush stained her cheeks. "It might have crossed my mind that the two of you would suit."

"Lady Anne is my friend, but nothing more than that." He tweaked one of her curls, a grin rising to his lips. "For sisters who are notorious for matchmaking, you're rather bad at it, you know."

She toyed with the folds of his cravat with her eyes still lowered. "What about Lady Pamela Fielding?"

"Lady Pamela Fielding!" He threw back his head in a laugh. "Good Lord, has that bit of gossip made it into my own house?"

"Abby's sister in London wrote to her about it. She says Lady Pamela is very fashionable and beautiful—"

"I've never looked twice at Lady Pamela Fielding, I promise you. There's not a drop of truth to that rumor."

"There isn't?"

"No, love. Not a single drop."

"Oh, well...that's good, then, because I'm certain she must be dreadful."

"She is, indeed." But the last thing he wanted to talk about when he had Helena in his arms was Lady Pamela. He dragged a fingertip over her lower lip. "I can't let you go, Helena. I want you to stay here with us forever. I want to marry you, sweetheart. Do you suppose the Templeton family has room for another countess?"

"I want that too, Adrian, so much, but what about Euphemia?" She let out a shaky breath. "If I stay here, she'll be all alone once my youngest sister Tilly goes, and I can't bear for her to be left—"

"Shh. We'll work something out with Euphemia, I promise it, but until we do, you and the boys and I will all go to Herefordshire together. We can marry there, if you like."

"You'd leave Hawke's Run, Adrian?" She slid her

arms around his neck, and rested her forehead against his. "Y—you'd do that, for *me*?"

He cupped her neck and held her close, his lips in her hair. "My dearest Helena, don't you understand? There isn't a single thing in the world I wouldn't do for you."

EPILOGUE

"Ryan, Etienne?" Adrian pounded up the back staircase, rounded the corner into the entryway and stopped short. "Oh, there you are."

"Good morning, papa!" Both boys sang out at once, identical angelic smiles on their faces.

Adrian's eyes narrowed on his sons. They were standing on either side of the closed entryway door, seeming like nothing so much as a pair of lookouts—or perhaps a pair of matching nutcrackers.

Those sweet smiles, however...he'd seen those particular smiles before, and always right before some ungodly chaos broke out. "What are you two up to?"

"Nothing at all, papa!" The boys sang out again.

"And we don't know where Mama is," Ryan added.

Mama. For months after he and Helena married, the boys had persisted in calling her "Miss Templeton." It had made his heart sink every time, as no one aside from Sophie herself could have been as much of a mother to Ryan and Etienne as Helena was, but every time it happened Helena only smiled, shook her head, and said, "Give them time, Adrian."

Time, as was the case with so many things, had wrought the change he'd hoped for. Occasionally Helena was still "Miss Templeton," but more often than not now, she was "Mama."

Except he hadn't asked them where Helena was, had he? Not yet, anyway. "How curious, Ryan, that you should be so quick to deny any knowledge of Mama's whereabouts when I didn't even ask after her."

"Well, she's not outside, so there's no reason for you to go out—ouch, Etienne!" Ryan glared at his brother, who'd just elbowed him hard in the ribs. "That hurt!"

"We weren't supposed to say anything! You're tattling it, Ryan!"

"I *didn't* tattle it! I never said a word about the alder tree!"

The alder tree! "Good Lord, don't tell me she's gone up that tree?" Helena had been muttering about mistletoe for days, as The St. Mary's Ladies' Benevolent Society Christmas Fete was only a few weeks away. She'd been made the head of the decorations committee this year, after Lady Codswaddle was dethroned in a unanimous vote.

He'd seen what was coming, of course, and had absolutely forbidden her to climb that blasted tree, but once Helena set her mind to a thing, nothing less than an act of God would deter her. "Devil take it."

"You shouldn't curse, papa," Etienne scolded. "Mama doesn't like it."

Well then, he and Helena were even so far this

morning, weren't they? "Come on, boys, let's go get her down."

"Yes, let's!" Rather than showing even a shred of remorse for having given Helena's secret away, the boys scurried joyously after him, chasing him through the door and down the drive, the frigid morning air whipping bright color into their cheeks.

He caught sight of her well before they reached the end of the drive, in part because she looked like some exotic winter bird, her blue cloak like bright plumage against the backdrop of the somber gray sky above, but also because of the round bundles of mistletoe sailing through the air and hitting the ground beneath the tree.

"Helena! What the devil do you think you're doing? Get down from there at once!"

She peered down at him through the dark branches, a bundle of mistletoe caught in her fist. "But I haven't finished yet."

"You are most assuredly finished, my lady. I'm warning you, Helena. Either come down from there at once, or I'm coming up to fetch you myself."

There was an exasperated huff, then the thorny bundle of mistletoe landed at his feet. "There's no need for *that*, I assure you. I'm nearly done. If you come up here now, you'll only slow me down."

"That's *it*, madam. Stay where you are." He braced his foot on one of the thicker branches near the bottom and caught hold of another one above his head.

"Hurrah!" The boys cried out gleefully. "Papa's going up the tree!"

Helena's head popped back into sight with her

lips turned down in a frown. "For pity's sake, Adrian, you're the most stubborn man alive."

"Then we're well matched, are we not, my lady?"

"What do you intend to do when you get up here? Carry me down on your back?"

"If that's what it takes to get you out of this bloody tree, then yes, and I warn you that once I have you down, I'm going to have the gardeners remove this cursed thing."

"What? But it has the nicest mistletoe in all of Steeple Barton!"

"Yes, well I'm very sorry for it, but as my wife can't seem to stay out of this tree, I haven't any other choice than to remove it." He'd nearly reached her now, just a few more branches and he'd have her.

There was another huff from above him. "Your wife is perfectly capable of making her way up this tree, and back down again, my lord. I've done it a dozen times."

"That, Helena, is precisely the problem." He was nearly there, just another few branches... "There! I've got you." He curled his arm around her waist, holding her carefully between his chest and the trunk of the tree.

"Where, my lord, will we get our mistletoe if you have the tree removed?"

"This may surprise you, Lady Hawke, but I don't give a damn about mistletoe. If the Benevolent Ladies insist upon having kissing balls, they'll have to start climbing trees themselves."

"Why, you awful man. Don't say you mean to send poor Lady Goodall up a tree."

It was meant as a scold, but the corners of her lips were twitching, and her eyes, more a blue than gray today, because of her cloak—were twinkling. He couldn't help but press a kiss to her lips, which resulted in a chorus of boyish giggles drifting up from the base of the tree.

"Perhaps not Lady Goodall," he allowed. "Or Lady Anne, as I believe Montgomery might object to it." Lady Anne had recently married a viscount, and the two of them were happily settled at Montgomery's country estate near Oxford, but Lord Codswaddle might be perfectly happy to see his wife sent up a tree.

"Husbands *do* seem to object to this sort of thing, don't they?" Helena let out a theatrical sigh.

"What, to the wives they adore scaling trees and risking their necks so Goodall Abbey can be smothered in kissing balls? They do rather, yes."

"Oh, but this mistletoe isn't for Goodall Abbey, my lord. This is for the kissing balls for Hawke's Run."

"Hawke's Run!" He let out a groan. "Don't tell me Goodall Abbey's flooded again, and we're to host the fete this year!" If that was the case, he'd do what he must, of course, but he'd been looking forward to spending a quiet Christmas with just the boys and Helena, especially as Tilly and Euphemia were meant to spend the New Year with them.

"No, these aren't for the fete at all. We've finished all the kissing balls for the fete already. These are *private* kissing balls, my lord, for us, alone."

"Private kissing balls?" That sounded a great deal more intriguing. "I see. Where do you intend to hang these private kissing balls, my lady?"

"Well, I thought we might start by hanging one over our bed."

"That *is* a good idea." He nuzzled her neck, a growl rumbling in his chest. "Anywhere else?"

"Yes. One from the mantel in our bedchamber, and perhaps we should fix one to the bronze lantern in the bathing room, above the bath."

"The *bath*? Dear God." A low, tortured groan slipped from his lips. "I was wrong. I *do* give a damn about kissing balls, after all. Anywhere else?"

"Yes, one last place."

"Mmm." He dragged his lips up her neck to her ear. "Where?"

"I think you'll especially like this idea, my lord."

He groaned again, his hands tightening around her waist. "Will I? Tell me, then."

"We must hang one from the rafters in the stables, right over the cat pen. I'd quite like another litter of kittens."

He paused in his exploration of her neck. "Kittens?"

"Yes, my lord. Kittens," she said, shaking with suppressed laughter.

"You're a wicked tease, Lady Hawke." He chuckled, and pressed a soft kiss behind her ear.

She smiled up at him, her arms stealing around his neck. "How in the world do you ever intend to get us down from this tree?"

"The same way we went up, my lady." He dropped another kiss on her lips. "One limb at a time."

ALSO BY ANNA BRADLEY

ABOUT THE AUTHOR

Anna Bradley writes steamy, sexy Regency historical romance—think garters, fops and riding crops! Readers can get in touch with Anna via her webpage at http://www.annabradley.net. Anna lives with her husband and two children in Portland, OR, where people are delightfully weird and love to read.

CPSIA information can be obtained
at www.ICGtesting.com
Printed in the USA
BVHW050204051222
653455BV00004B/20